The
Giant Rat of Sumatra

THE BAKER STREET MYSTERIES

BOOK 2

The
Giant Rat of Sumatra

JAKE & LUKE
THOENE

MOORINGS
Nashville, Tennessee
A Division of the Ballantine Publishing Group,
Random House, Inc.

Book 2
The Baker Street Mysteries
THE GIANT RAT OF SUMATRA

Copyright © 1995 by Jacob Brock Thoene and Thomas Luke Thoene

Published in association with the Literary Agency of
Alive Communications, Inc.,
1465 Kelly Johnson Blvd., Suite 320, Colorado Springs, CO 80920.

Library of Congress Cataloging-in-Publication Data
Thoene, Jake.
    The giant rat of Sumatra / Jake & Luke Thoene. — 1st ed.
        p.   cm. — (The Baker Street mysteries ; bk. 2)
    Summary: When priceless gifts for Queen Victoria's Jubilee begin to
disappear from the Tower of London, Sherlock Holmes calls on the Baker
Street Brigade to help solve the mystery.
    ISBN 0-345-39560-3
    [1. Robbers and outlaws—Fiction. 2. London (England)—Fiction.
3. Mystery and detective stories.] I. Thoene, Luke. II. Title.
III. Series: Thoene, Jake. Baker Street mysteries ; bk. 2.
PZ7. T35655Gi   1995
[Fic]—dc20   95-25074
                                                                  CIP
                                                                   AC

First Edition: October 1995

10   9   8   7   6   5   4   3   2   1

*This book is dedicated to
Bodie Thoene, our mother.
Her knowledge and guidance
have made these stories
a joy for us.*

Thanks and blessings,

Jake and Luke

THE TOWER
1890

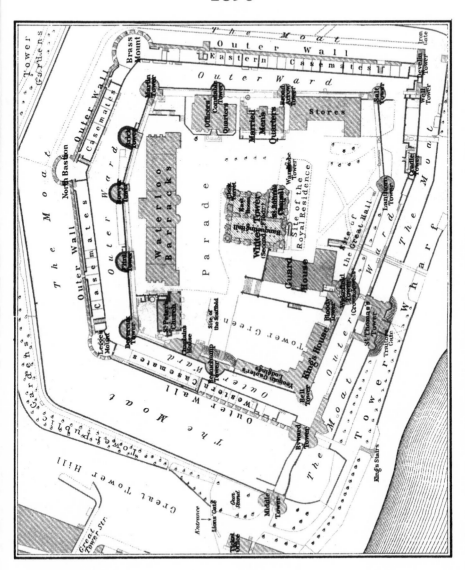

PROLOGUE

THE WALLS of the Tower of London rose in a ghostly silhouette beside the Thames River. The moist air above the river and the coal-black darkness of the night absorbed all the bustle and clatter of the great city until all was unnaturally still. Illuminated only at distant intervals by dim and flickering torches hung from rusty iron sconces in the stone, the fortress appeared unreal, as in a dream . . . or a nightmare.

All who lay sleeping inside the castle slept deeply, peacefully. They were protected both by the heavy beams of the barred gates and by the guards who walked their rounds, alert and cautious.

"You take the low road and I'll take the high road and I'll be t' London afore ye," Richard Cahlee belted as he strolled along the Outer Ward. Cahlee was sixty-one years of age, retired to the life of a yeoman warder in the Tower of London after an honorable discharge from Her Majesty's Royal Navy after reaching the rank of chief bosun's mate on the HMS *Dunley*.

When Cahlee's age and portly figure made him unfit for further active duty at sea, he had applied to join the Warders. Guardians of Her Majesty's Royal Palace and Fortress, the yeoman warders accepted Cahlee on the basis of his distinguished career, his undying devotion to the queen and the fact that he had no family or relatives.

"Quiet down!" a voice hissed from the darkness. Cahlee's fellow sentry on the wall of the Inner Ward objected to his noisy singing.

"Don't tell me t' quiet doon," Cahlee mumbled to himself. "Young oopstart soldier, tellin' me what t' do." Nevertheless, his volume trailed off as he withdrew a flask from the inside of his uniform jacket and gulped down a quarter of the whiskey inside. Still defiantly humming the tune, he walked on to the south wall of the Tower.

As he turned the corner past the Bell Tower and entered Water Lane, a cool breeze touched his face and brought him the foul smell of the river. Cahlee compensated for the dank mustiness by lighting a large Studard and Sons cigar.

Easing his bulk down to a seat on a bench below the Bloody Tower, Cahlee loosened his collar stay and puffed contentedly. Though it was lonely on his night patrol, he enjoyed relaxing near the south wall where the gentle sound of the water lapped at the steps of Traitors' Gate. This opening through the outer wall of the Tower to the river was secured against unlawful entry by an iron grate lowered across the channel. A great many prisoners had been brought to the fortress by this gate, never to see the outside world again.

Cahlee's tight wool uniform, combined with all the walking, had made him hot and tired and he leaned back against the cool stones of the wall to relax. "I'll not be bullied by some oopstart fresh out of nappies," he growled, still angry at having been told to be quiet. His mood improved as he recounted to himself his fighting days on the *Dunley*. With the sound of the splashing waves and swirl of air, he found himself at sea again, running down a rogue frigate suspected of smuggling black-market goods. He saluted the memory with another sip from the flask. "Those were th' days," he sighed again, dropping the last of his cigar. He rose unsteadily to his feet and walked on.

The sweat on his pudgy neck made him shiver as it cooled and he hitched up his coat. He began humming again as he thought of proudly standing on the deck for the last thirteen years. Cahlee wondered, as he often did, how it was that he could be chief bosun's mate of a ship for thirteen years and still have to take orders from the youngest and dumbest commissioned officers. He had seen four captains come and go, but he remained constant. And though he wondered why he could never achieve an officer's station, he knew the answer: he had not come from a rich family and had not attended the naval academy, but instead enlisted at the age of sixteen, looking for adventure. So he worked hard, finding himself promoted frequently. He soon stood by the captain himself at the highest rank among the enlisted men. But the world of commissioned officers was reserved for those properly educated, of noble families.

"And no doubt a bit of the silver changed hands, too," Cahlee said aloud, startling himself as his words echoed hollowly off the stones. He reached the end of his route and turned back toward the west. As he passed Traitors' Gate once more, he paused and picked up the butt of his cigar, which had burned itself out on the cobblestones. "Queen wouldn't like to find I was relaxin' on the job," he muttered, tossing the stub into the water.

Cahlee was turning from the gate when he heard a rasping noise that made him pause. He turned back, looking through the closed iron grill, or portcullis, and up the shimmering channel that led back to the blackness of the river. He picked up a candle lantern that hung on the wall nearby and, holding it aloft, peered into the darkness. Close to the gate he saw a small circle of churning water.

Walking down the first two of the docking steps, murky water slapping just inches below, Cahlee strained to see the cause of the strange disturbance. At that same moment something surfaced just a few yards away. It let out a blast of air that turned the surrounding water into a fine mist. A knobby crown tapered to the point of a large, wicked snout. The thing was larger than a man's head and had two eyes that seemed to burn with evil in the reflection of the lantern. It turned toward Cahlee, piercing him with its malevolent gaze.

"What the . . . Help!" Cahlee yelled, dropping the lantern and stumbling backward, trying to distance himself from the huge creature. He slipped on the wet steps and fell, hitting his head on the cobblestones. The lantern clattered and bounced, the candle hissing as it went out. Shouts of alarm came from within the Tower walls and several men rushed to Cahlee's aid, just as he lost consciousness.

ONE

THE YEAR WAS 1887. London was the thriving capital of a British Empire that encircled the globe. It was the year of Queen Victoria's Golden Jubilee, marking her fifty years on the throne. To honor her, priceless treasures, gold and jewels and other gifts, were brought from all over the world. They were to be guarded and temporarily stored at the Tower of London, the most famous fortress in all of England, perhaps in all the world.

Two enormously high walls, studded with over twenty solid stone towers, provided the castle's strength. Behind these impenetrable barriers was a completely self-sufficient village, including an army barracks, food storage for a year, several storehouses of weapons, and a royal prison. The Tower of London also contained two chapels and the Jewel House, in which were kept the crown jewels of England.

In the late nineteenth century, the Tower remained a fully operational military post, housing many soldiers. Among these were the legendary yeoman warders, nicknamed the beefeaters, keepers of the Tower. Also, it was home to the ravens, who had lived there for centuries. It was said that if the ravens should leave the Tower for any reason, the fortress would fall, along with England and the monarchy.

The Tower was a force to be reckoned with. So imposing was its appearance that outside of the Peasants' Revolt in the year 1381, the Tower had never officially been attacked. And by 1887, the Tower had taken on the additional roll of a national monument, representing the strength of the British Empire. Thick with history, it contained the legends of ghosts, mysteries, and murders.

Large vessels flying colorful flags crowded the anchorage along the river Thames in front of the Tower. A warship bearing the Imperial German banner was peacefully moored alongside a steamer under the blue and white emblem of Argentina. These and many others were welcomed by those displaying the three crosses of Britain's Union Jack. Their launches brought high diplomats ashore to Tower Wharf as the cannons of the saluting battery fired countless blasts of recognition. The arriving visitors brought gifts of all sorts—perfumes, exotic spices, expensive clothing, even unusual animals, but many brought priceless jewels.

A country's pride and admiration for Queen Victoria was expressed by its gift, often a unique gem. Rubies, diamonds, and emeralds, many set into gold, traveled from all over the world to be presented to the queen. Representatives from many nations came to honor her and perhaps to buy her favor should they need help in the future.

They came to the Tower of London, the huge fortress begun by William the Conqueror in 1066 that was now recognized as a symbol of the entire country. The intricate masonry revealed the pride of the workmen and the people. The quality of the stone illustrated their desire to be the best. The thickness, height, and strength of the walls demonstrated to all enemies of England's monarchy that it was a force to be reckoned with, and confirmed to all friends that they would be safe there.

Away from the river, on the landward side, carriages lined the entranceway as lords, ladies, dukes, duchesses, and other English nobility came from their country mansions to meet the foreign diplomats. Smaller, poorer countries sent their rulers; the larger ones sent princes or diplomats. All were admitted to the Tower to see Queen Victoria's private secretary, Sir Henry Ponsonby, and deliver their gifts.

———

"The war chief of the Zulu nation, Swiruli Mungu, presenting the Diamond of Shaka," the representative of the Lord Chamberlain's office announced.

A tall black man wearing a leopard skin over his formal cutaway coat walked forward. On a bright-red velvet pillow he carried an uncut diamond the size of an egg. Bowing deeply to an oil portrait of the queen that hung over the receiving table, he set the gift on the mahogany surface in front of Sir Henry Ponsonby.

"Mr. Privy Councilor," Mungu spoke with a deep, melodious voice as he bent to one knee, "a gift for Her Majesty from the people of Zululand. May she live to be honored again, in another fifty years. And may she reign fifty-times-fifty years." He rose, bowing again to the portrait.

"Her Majesty thanks you, Chief Mungu," Sir

Henry replied. The world-famous consulting detective, Sherlock Holmes, and Chief Yeoman Warder Walter Gladstone watched as another gift bearer was called from the ranks outside the greeting chamber. Also standing nearby was the tall, handsome Ronald Frith, at age forty the youngest captain in the Tower's detachment of guardsmen. Frith's father, Baron Mackenly Frith of Rochester, was also on hand. All four men watched the delivery of the gifts from foreign nations.

"We called you here because you don't miss a thing, Mr. Holmes," Gladstone said. As chief yeoman warder, the man in charge of all the Tower's watchmen, Gladstone was responsible for the safekeeping of the presents until they were formally accepted by the queen on the day of the Jubilee ceremony only a week away.

From the hall echoed the announcement, "Ambassador Nels Van Rorin of the Sunda Islands with the Suir Pearl . . ."

"I assume that if something *is* wrong with the security measures, you would be able to point it out immediately," Baron Frith said grumpily to Holmes, inhaling a pinch of snuff from his silver snuffbox. "Deuced bother, all these formalities. Why can't Her Majesty just lock up the gifts and be done with it?"

"Protocol," Gladstone answered, but Lord Frith sneezed into a lace handkerchief, drowning out the reply.

"Protocol," Gladstone repeated. "It would be a scandal of the highest magnitude if anything happened to the tributes before they had been formally received."

"Quite right, gentlemen," Holmes agreed, his quick eyes darting around the room. "Though at present I detect no problems in your arrangements."

"Well, that's a relief," Gladstone sighed. "This is all so important that . . ."

"I would like to see where the gifts are kept after their reception here," Holmes interrupted. "If anything is to be stolen, the thief surely would not do it here."

"Quite right, Mr. Holmes. Right this way." Gladstone turned and led the group toward the door.

Walking out of the Waterloo Block where the diplomats made their presentations, Holmes and Gladstone and the Friths entered the Broad Walk, which lies between the barracks and the White Tower, started in 1078 by William the Conqueror. The White Tower was a castle in its own right, standing four stories tall with thick brick walls and large windows. Its name came from the whitewash applied to the stone used in its construction.

The chief warder led the way into the White Tower where the Great Hall was to house the Jubilee gifts. "Well, Mr. Holmes, what do you think?" asked Captain Ronald Frith.

"Gentlemen, this is ridiculous!" Holmes exclaimed. "On our walk to this chamber I have seen no guards, in the battlements no guards are stationed, and this door has but one bolt on it. I fail to see that any precautionary measures have been taken at all!"

Lord Frith looked astonished at the force of Holmes's attack. His son appeared to be amused by the outburst.

"Mr. Holmes!" Gladstone said defensively. "You neglect to notice that no one could get over the outer perimeter wall, much less go unnoticed through the inner courtyard! Truth be told, Mr. Holmes, I brought you here to get your approval of our security, not to have you change our rules or rebuild the Tower!"

"Indeed, Mr. Gladstone?" Holmes snorted. "Then shall I be off? Or would you have me find the weaknesses and report them to you so that nothing *will* happen?"

"I suppose that, if you feel it necessary . . ."

"Good!" Holmes shouted. "Then I must go now to make arrangements to test your defenses. I will not tell you how, but I guarantee I will prove to you that your protection here is nothing of the sort."

"Well, I . . ." Gladstone looked for support from Lord Frith, but the nobleman also was shocked and speechless.

"Excellent, I'll be off then." Holmes paused. "Oh, one more thing, Gladstone. Had you a strange occurrence at the waterfront at approximately 11:30 last evening . . . an occurrence where one of the participants was left unconscious?"

"Why, that's amazing, Mr. Holmes! How did you know?"

"Never mind how, Gladstone! What were the circumstances?"

Gladstone made a face that spoke of his reluctance to discuss the subject. Then making up his mind to cooperate fully, he squared his shoulders and explained. "One of our warders, I'm embarrassed to say, is fond of his whiskey. Last night he became drunk and slipped on the wet steps of Traitors' Gate. You are wrong about one thing: the man was not unconscious; he died from his injuries."

"Ah, very well," Holmes said in a quieter tone. "But in future, keep nothing from me, no matter how trivial it may seem to you!"

"But Mr. Holmes," Captain Frith blurted. "How *did* you know about the man at all? Apart from Chief

Gladstone, myself, and one or two others, no one has been informed of the incident. Why, not even my father here was told. Do you have spies already at work within these walls?"

Holmes shook his head, then somewhat immodestly elevated his long, thin nose with the pleasure of demonstrating his sleuthing ability. "Elementary," he replied. "Upon entering the Tower today, I observed some slight scratch marks from the heels of a pair of men's boots leading away up the cobblestones outside the Bloody Tower . . . marks of the type left when a body is dragged away by the arms. Such marks are often found at the scene of a crime."

"But what of the time, Mr. Holmes? How did you know when it happened?" asked Lord Frith.

"Simple, sir! The lantern hanging by the gate had obviously recently been dropped, judging by the fresh scrapes in the metal that were still far brighter than even a few days' exposure to our London fogs would permit. That the heel scrapes and the damage to the lantern could be unconnected seemed too great a coincidence."

"Yes, go on."

"Looking 'round, I spotted a candle in the water by the water-gate steps, of the same type as used in the lantern. Presumably it dislodged when the lantern dropped. Realize that the candles used here burn approximately one-half inch every hour. Therefore, knowing that darkness, last night, fell at half past eight and the candle was burned down in height approximately one-and-one-half inches, then we can assume that the candle went out sometime between eleven and midnight."

"That's amazing, Mr. Holmes! How do you do it?"

Captain Frith asked. "Is it a sort of game or parlor trick? Or were you born with second sight?"

"It is neither a trick nor an inborn gift, I can assure you. I learned these skills by much practice in observing. Observation is always the key. Now," Holmes said as he turned toward the stairs, "I have other business to attend to. Mr. Gladstone, I appreciate your invitation to dine with you tonight. I accept. I will join you at eight, if that is convenient. If you'll excuse me, gentlemen?"

TWO

DANNY WIGGINS, HIS dark eyes taking in all the bustling activity on Tower Hill, watched as a lovely young lady in a high-collared, ankle-length burgundy dress stepped down from her carriage into the street outside the Tower. He thought she was one of the more attractive of the many upper-class English visitors to the Tower that day. The carriages of the nobility vied with those of the foreign diplomats bringing gifts for the queen.

"Hey, Wiggins," a voice yelled from up the avenue toward Trinity Square. Danny jumped, looking around to see who had caught him staring at the young woman.

"Stop dreaming and sell your papers!"

It was Danny's friend, fellow street rat and partner in adventure, Peachy Carnehan. The fair-skinned Peachy shouted from across the street, "Blimey! If you like the lady that much, sell her the news!"

"Leave off paying attention to me and sell your own papers!" Danny yelled back. Both boys laughed and returned to hawking copies of the *Daily Standard* to the gents, swells, shoppers, and clerks.

"Extra! Read all about it!" Peachy belted. "Victoria's bash brings big booty! Only a tanner; sixpence for all the news!" Peachy was twelve, red-haired, and freckled. Danny was thirteen and nearly Peachy's opposite in looks with dark hair, dark complexion, and stocky build. They were also opposite in disposition, given Danny's thoughtfulness and Peachy's temper.

"Hey, Duff!" Danny yelled. "Bring me some more of the news, mate!" Standing equally distant from Danny and Peachy, as was always their arrangement, Duff Bernard stood guard over a stack of papers that totaled all three of their shares for the afternoon.

"Cheerio, Danny," Duff called back, hefting the entire stack, sixty pounds of newspapers, and toting them toward Danny. Duff was fifteen and quite large for his age, but he was also slow in his thinking. Danny always said that Duff would never make a sale and even if he did, the customer would shortchange him every time. So Danny and Peachy took it on themselves to sell Duff's share as long as he held the heap for all of them.

"Here, Danny," Duff said. "I brought them. We had one hundred twenty-three when we started, but there's only thirty-one left . . . is that good?"

"Crikey!" Danny said, always amazed at Duff's ability to recall odd things. His friend might not be quick, but at some things he was a wizard! "Of course it's good, Duff! Once we run out we can go back to school and play some tick-tack-toe before we go to bed."

The three boys, all orphans, lived at Waterloo Road Ragged School, a boarding school run by Christian folk who took in some of the thousands of otherwise homeless London children. The three friends got two meals a day, an education, and a place to sleep, but they sold papers for spending money and to help out with the expenses of the school.

"But can we eat first?" Duff asked, unhappy wrinkles clouding his usually cheerful face. Even though Duff had a sticky bun and a pint of tea with sugar not fifteen minutes before, he was still concerned about getting enough food for the day. The size of Duff's appetite was similar to that of the large dog with which he shared a last name.

But Danny didn't answer, his attention back on the gentlewoman who had arrived in the carriage. "Danny," Duff begged again, "we are gonna eat again before bed, what?"

"Give over, Duff! Not now! Oy, Peachy," Danny called, "come quick!"

Peachy hurriedly made change for a shilling and then trotted down the street looking annoyed.

"What is it?" Peachy complained. "I'm almost sold out, see? And the swells are buyin' for their ladies on accounta the news about the queen. I've got a good line of patter goin', so can't it wait?"

"No, Peachy, it can't wait. The princess over there is getting cased for a pull."

"What? You mean somebody's tryin' to lift her purse right here?"

"That's exactly what I mean," Danny retorted. "Cool the square-rigged gent flexin' his knuckles."

Peachy followed the direction indicated by Danny's outstretched arm. They watched as two men dressed formally in business suits and top hats followed the woman in single file toward the Tower entrance. Another man in a cloth cap and workman's overalls approached the procession from the front. To Danny's keen eye it was a classic setup worked by flimps . . . pickpockets.

"Peachy," Danny instructed, "stop the bagman! Duff," Danny said hurriedly, "here's what I need you to do."

The laborer strolling toward the woman seemed to stumble and bump into her, just as the thief immediately behind relieved her dress pocket of her purse. As the workingman tugged on his cloth cap and apologized to the lady, the dip, the one who made the pull, handed the pocketbook to the accomplice behind him. This last in line turned sharply away as if to cross the street and fade into the crowd, but came face to face with Peachy Carnehan. Peachy shoved the man in the center of his yellow silk waistcoat, knocking him down onto the street. The thief's shiny black top hat rolled into the gutter and landed on a heap of horse dung.

"Why, you clumsy little beggar, I'll burke you for fair!" threatened the man.

Just then Duff grabbed the thief by the collar with his right hand and jerked him halfway to his feet. Duff's big, muscular hand got a large bit of shirt collar, waistcoat, dress coat, and skin, making the man choke and flail his arms.

Danny seized the woman's pocketbook back from the man and yelled for a constable. "Sir," Danny began to a blue uniformed policeman who came running up, "this man . . ."

"I saw this little scoundrel lift that lady's purse," sputtered the thief as he dangled from Duff's grip. "I tried to get it back from them, but the rest of his mates jumped me."

Duff dropped the man back on the ground, where

he landed on top of hat and horse manure. "Liar!" he scolded. "Liar, liar, liar! We was selling the papers when Danny says I see a pick job, and . . ."

The patrolman looked very stern and the pickpocket nodded his agreement. "See, officer? They admit it!"

Peachy slapped his own forehead in disbelief. "Blimey, Duff! I can't believe you said that."

"What he means is," Danny tried to explain, "I saw these three men about to nab her money, see? So I says to Duff and Peachy here . . ."

"Save it lads, save it," the constable interrupted, comparing the ragged shoeless boys to the fashionably dressed man. "You save your tales for the magistrate. Give me no trouble now, I'm taking you boys in." The officer reached inside his tunic and withdrew a silver whistle on a chain and prepared to blow it.

"But sir . . . ," Peachy tried.

"Well done, constable," the thief said. "I'll just return this purse to its rightful owner," and he began to saunter toward the Tower gate as if to return the stolen property.

Just then an authoritative voice boomed from the crowd of onlookers that had formed. "Unhand those boys!" The audience parted and Sherlock Holmes stepped through.

"Eh? Oh, it's you, Mr. Holmes," the policeman said, surprised at the interference. "What was that?"

"I said, unhand those boys! I was witness to the entire event and the true criminal is now departing with the stolen goods." Holmes extended his long arm and pointed a slender index finger at the back of the departing rogue.

"You mean that man?"

"Quite!" Holmes concluded abruptly. "Now hurry and catch him." The officer let go of Peachy and Danny and ran toward where he had last seen the crook push between a carriage and a hansom cab. Turning to the boys, Holmes said, "Nicely done, Wiggins. I can see your observational skills are improving."

"Thank you, Mr. Holmes," Danny replied. "It's too bad I couldn't make it turn out right like you, though."

"Tut, Wiggins! The setup to catch a criminal must be as carefully planned as the crime, or the perpetrator may have wits enough to escape at the last moment. It reminds me of the tragedy of the Kalimantan Goose." Holmes stared off for a moment, his eyes flickering toward the imposing bulk of the Royal Mint building, recalling some unusual mystery in his past. Then shaking himself free from the reverie he continued, "In any case, I have some work for you three. Come to Baker Street when you finish your business here. There may be a shilling in it for you."

"Yes sir, Mr. Holmes," Peachy said. "Glad to oblige."

"Anything you need," Danny added.

"Will there be tea and biscuits?" Duff asked.

Holmes smiled as he headed off and hailed a cab. Closing the apron doors, he sat down in the two-wheeled cart and tapped with his walking stick on the ceiling of the cab to show he was ready. The driver pulled away from the curb.

The boys saw the constable heading back their way. The man looked miserable. "The buzzer took to flight," he panted as he neared the boys. "Bloke dropped the purse as I chased him. He kicked it into the bushes and now I can't find the blooming thing."

Peachy rolled his eyes.

"Well," Danny said. "I say whoever finds the pocketbook first gets the pleasure of returning it to the owner!" They all began looking at once.

It was just a few seconds when a pleased voice called, "Got it!"

Danny looked at Peachy, Peachy stared at the constable, and the officer gazed at Duff as the large boy started toward the lady with her purse in his hands, brushing the dirt off as he went. "Cripes, Peachy," Danny said. "Let's finish with these papers before Duff comes back to show us his reward."

The brass knocker on the door of 221-B Baker Street clattered as Danny let it fall against the panel. Peachy and Duff stood behind him as they waited for Mrs. Hudson, Sherlock Holmes's housekeeper, to answer the door.

The boys heard a crash inside and the sound of raised voices. These noises were followed by the hollow clopping of footsteps tromping down the stairs. An instant later the door flew open. It was not the short, plump Mrs. Hudson who confronted them, but the tall, lean form of Holmes himself. The private investigator was wearing a mouse-gray dressing gown over his shirt and trousers. Danny noticed that the sleeves were flecked with bits of chipped pottery, but Holmes seemed not to be aware that anything was wrong.

"Come in, come in, my little wharf rats! What took so long?" The detective spoke excitedly, in the manner he showed only when an interesting case was underway.

"Crikey, Mr. Holmes," Peachy said, trying to peer around the sleuth into the entryway, "what happened in there? We heard some right dodgy noises."

"Oh, nothing important," Holmes replied, dismissing the question with a wave of his hand. "Just another experiment."

"Nothing important?" Mrs. Hudson objected. Her voice came shrilly down the stairs, growing louder and more strident as she descended the flight of steps. "Let me tell you what this great detective did in his experiment: he's baked a fine mixture of cement and horse manure into the last and the best teapot he owns. And it's not destroying his own property that bothers me, it's that tomorrow he'll cry and complain until he gets his tea!"

"Pay her no mind, boys," Holmes instructed as he swept past the housekeeper, leading the way back upstairs. Mrs. Hudson gasped disgustedly and stormed off into the kitchen. "Come up to my sitting room and I'll tell you what I have in store for you."

To enter the parlor, Danny and the others had to step over the remains of a broken teapot in the middle of the carpet. Holmes paid no attention to the shattered crockery or the other remains of his research trial. "Make yourselves comfortable," he proposed to them.

"What's all this, then?" Peachy asked, impatient for an explanation. "I mean, why couldn't you tell us at the Tower?"

"Carnehan, the assignment I have for you concerns the Tower. It could also involve onlookers to today's scene with the pickpocket. What I have to tell is very important, but must be kept a secret from everyone." The detective paused and looked each boy in the face until he got nods of agreement from all three.

Even Duff seemed to understand the seriousness of the request . . . seemed to, that is, until he asked, "Why would you want to drink horse dung and concrete?" Danny and Holmes smiled, while Peachy just shook his head.

"I'll vouch for him," Danny said. "He won't breathe a word to no one."

Satisfied, Holmes resumed. "I was called to the Tower by the chief yeoman warder. He has hired me as a private security consultant."

"What's that mean, Mr. Holmes?" Peachy asked.

"It means, Carnehan, that my efforts to educate the authorities about scientific methods of crime detection and prevention are beginning to show fruit. My services are requested in order to prevent a crime from happening; clearly a better situation than having to solve one that has already taken place."

"That's all well and good, but where do we come in?" Peachy persisted.

"Patience, Carnehan! Frankly, I think Chief Warder Gladstone wanted my presence to impress Lord Frith of Her Majesty's reception committee that everything was already safe and secure. However . . ." There was a long, unbroken pause in which Danny heard Duff's stomach rumble.

"Go on, sir," Danny urged.

"I have detected certain weaknesses just by my stroll through the grounds today; weaknesses that may provide opportunity for crime and political scandal."

"Like what, sir?" Danny asked.

"For instance, during the day there are no guards present at the storage room in which the diplomatic gifts are housed. Warder Gladstone is reluctant to admit that the Tower is vulnerable. I intend to prove that it is."

"So what are we to do about it?" Peachy asked again.

"I've decided to hire you as my spies. You three are to enter the Tower before the day is through and hide yourselves until after dark when you can observe all guard locations, activities, and habits. Basically, gentlemen, look for ways in. Take notes in your minds, then report back to me tomorrow."

"Cor," Peachy said, his freckles lighting up with excitement. "That's a great-sounding plan. But how are we supposed to skip from the crushers, much less stay on the wing all night?"

"A valid point, Carnehan, but not to worry. There are tours into the fortress every quarter of an hour, leading through the Wakefield Tower where the crown jewels are stored. These tours are open to any of the public willing to pay, the money for which I will supply. Somewhere along the tour, drop to the end of the group . . ."

Danny interrupted, excited with the idea. "And find a lurk somewhere until they leave, right? Then it's cat-an'-mouse till break of day. If we stay free, then we . . . that is, you . . . win."

Holmes smiled. "Precisely, Wiggins. If you can elude their security, then we will have proven that additional efforts are needed." Danny and Peachy congratulated each other on being on another case with Sherlock Holmes. The detective let their enthusiasm simmer down before he held up a cautioning finger. "One more thing, gentlemen: should you be discovered and detained, say nothing about me or this plan to anyone save Chief Warder Gladstone, and only then if he is alone. Understood? For the early part of the evening, I will be at the Gladstone home, but if you are apprehended that early, then you are not the sly wharf rats I take you for."

The three nodded and waited for their next instructions.

Then Duff said, "No tea and biscuits? Will we miss supper at school, too?"

"I have taken the liberty of contacting your school's headmaster, Mr. Ingram. If you are willing to assist me, he has given his permission for your absence. Now, as there will be neither time nor place to eat once inside, I'll have Mrs. Hudson make some dinner for you."

Danny, Peachy, and Duff went out of the parlor and up the next flight of stairs to Holmes's bathroom to wash up. Holmes settled back in his favorite wing-backed chair and lit his long-stemmed churchwarden pipe before calling out, "Mrs. Hudson! The boys and I have a very busy night ahead of us and need an early dinner. So might you prepare something in a hurry?"

"Yes, Mr. Holmes!" the housekeeper called back from downstairs, sounding very annoyed.

"Oh, and Mrs. Hudson?" the detective continued, sending a spiral of blue smoke up toward the globe of the gas lamp. "Could you brew us up some of your nice tea as well?"

THREE

GRAY CLOUDS HOVERED over the queue that stretched halfway from Tower Hill to the Byward Tower entrance of the Tower of London. Women wearing long dresses made extra full by multiple layers of white petticoats fanned themselves as the line crept slowly forward. Duff scuffed his boots impatiently and Peachy gave a frustrated sigh. "Come on, then. We haven't got all day." It was already late afternoon and the last showing of the royal jewels had already been announced.

The queue finally shifted the boys to the head of the line, where a man in a makeshift wooden shack said, "That'll be tuppence apiece, lads. 'Ear all about the ghosts of the young princes who was murdered in their sleep. See the famous ar-mee-ment of 'Enry the Eighth an' the fab-oo-lus crown joo-ells."

Danny reached in his pocket, pulling out the folded handkerchief that contained an assortment of useful little bits of junk he'd collected. "I've got them here somewhere," he said, picking through string, wire, a small file, and a pair of matches. He retrieved the three tuppence coins, placing them in front of the ticket seller.

"Cheers, boys, enjoy the show," the baldheaded man said as he picked up each coin in his stubby fingers and rapped it against the countertop. He leaned over and said in a conspiratorial whisper, "Watch out for that Anne Boleyn! They say she still roams the castle at night lookin' for 'er 'ead."

Peachy knew the man was having them on and he laughed to himself that someone with a bit of dried gravy stuck in his scraggly gray beard should try to be scary.

But Duff stared at the man's raised eyebrows and raised his own in response. With a frightened look on his face, he tugged at Danny's sleeve. "Danny, you told me there weren't no ghosts around here."

Peachy blew out a heavy breath of disbelief and disgust. "Crikey, Duff! Don't let him gull you with no glocky tale! You know there ain't no such thing as ghosts." Raising his pug nose till it pointed with accusation at the ticket seller, he added, "Is there?"

The vendor shrugged and sniffed. "Never mind me, then," he said. "Believe what you like, but don't wander off into no dungeons or you may never come out alive." He sat back in his chair, snickering to himself and scratching his fat belly through his shirt.

Duff still remained unconvinced. "Danny," he asked, "you sure there won't be no ghosts? I don't want to see no ghosts, Danny. I wouldn't like it."

Danny said kindly, "There are no ghosts, Duff, but if you're scared, you can go home now. You don't have to come."

Duff puckered his face in thought till it looked like a raisin, then said, "I don't believe in no ghosts."

"Good," Danny said. "Now we can get on."

"Hear ye, hear ye," a yeoman warder dressed in a dark blue uniform announced. "All of ye who wish to join me on an adventure through the ages, step right this way." The guard, whose ears stuck out, removed a hat shaped like an upside-down mushroom and held it next to his chest where the initials *V* and *R* were embroidered. The chattering crowd followed as he marched proudly across the bridge that led through the main gate.

Danny and the others of Sherlock Holmes's little brigade of irregular troops joined the crowd. The three boys stayed at the rear of the mass as they entered Water Lane.

"Here in this very spot," the warder addressed the group, pointing to the corner tower just inside the gate, "called the Bell Tower, is where the famous Sir Thomas More was locked up by King Henry VIII. Thomas lived in the Tower for several months before old Henry finally done off with his head. He was a mean man, was old Henry, always chopping off the heads of those as didn't agree with him. It didn't matter if they was friends or wives. One cross word and lop them off, he did."

A shudder ran through the throng and was shared by Peachy, though he hoped no one noticed. Seeing Danny looking at him curiously, Peachy squared his shoulders and scowled.

The yeoman warder hunched over. Squinting his eyes, he said, "They say the ghost of Sir Thomas is still about. Only one of many haunts what makes their homes here." Peachy looked the other way, but the crowd leaned in as the guard said in a stage whisper, "In fact, right over there, next to Traitors' Gate, is where Sir Thomas's ghost was first spotted."

Danny felt a chill run down his spine as dead silence fell over the crowd.

"They say there's men as much as gave up their pension here at the Tower after seeing the ghost," the warder said spookily, "never to work here again." He looked around the group, trying to impress them with the intensity of the tale.

Danny thought how everyone from the ticket seller to the guards tried to make the Tower seem as scary as possible.

"Which brings us across to the Bloody Tower," the warder continued, pointing up at the inner wall. "It's a story of murder. Two boy princes, one born to be King Edward V, and his younger brother, were, by their cruel uncle's orders, locked in the Tower. They disappeared late one night. No one ever heard a sound, nor a soul saw anything." He paused. "But that next morning, they were gone without a trace."

Peachy's stomach began to flutter, as his heart pounded in his ears. Uneasy, he scuffed his boots, trying not to listen and trying to look completely unconcerned at the same time.

The guard stamped his foot and stood up straight. "Naturally, Uncle Richard, him as became King Richard III, could not escape judgment for his heinous crime. He himself was killed in battle not two years after." The warder dropped his voice, making everyone, including Peachy, lean in closer to hear the end of the story. "And it's said the ghosts of the young princes can still be seen in the window of the room where they were murdered." He spun around sharply with his arm extended and bellowed, "Right up there!"

Peachy jumped, but he did not think anyone noticed, since the entire crowd had been startled as well. An ooh emanated from the mob, which then began to chatter.

"Right this way," the yeoman warder instructed, "and I'll be showing you through the Wakefield Tower, where the queen's jewels are now kept."

"Peachy," Danny said softly, making Peachy jump again by grabbing his elbow. "This is where Mr. Holmes wanted us to spy a lurk."

Peachy was relieved to be reminded that they were there for a purpose . . . on business. Mr. Holmes surely would not be impressed to hear that he was afraid of ghost stories. Peachy made up his mind to concentrate on what Mr. Holmes had sent them to do.

The throng of people filtered after the guard, under the portcullis, whose iron spikes hung over their heads, and through the passage beneath the Bloody Tower. "We'll hang back until no one's looking," Peachy said. The three friends looked furtively around to see if anyone was watching, then stayed behind in the shadows under the heavy metal grate.

The warder's voice carried from a distance, inside the inner wall of the fortress. "Right there is the pen for the Tower ravens. The birds have the royal protection, but come and go as they wants. By tradition they are fed and sheltered here if they wish. Please do not molest the ravens, ladies and gentlemen. And up there, on Tower Green, is where many of royalty lost their heads to the ax."

"Come on," Peachy motioned, "let's go through here." He led the way back onto Water Lane, ducking around a corner of the Wakefield Tower and out of sight of the tour group. "Quick!" he urged. "Before anyone notices we're gone!"

———

The simple dinner that Chief Warder Gladstone's wife, Mary, prepared was met with delight by Holmes. "Obviously you enjoyed your time in the Orient with Walter, Mrs. Gladstone," Holmes said as he finished eating. "And you have gained from the experience." The chief warder had left the room for a moment.

"Why thank you, Mr. Holmes. I didn't realize that Walter had told you so much about his former posts."

"He has not," said Holmes with a cryptic smile. "Ah, Walter, so you've returned."

"Yes, Mr. Holmes," Walter replied as he took his seat. "Just going over the duty roster with Captain Frith. Now, where were we?"

"We were discussing jewel thefts of past."

"And attempted escapes," Mary added. "There is so much history here in the Tower," she said. "One almost feels as if it were still going on. Why, even our home here in the Constable Tower," she said, waving at the whitewashed stones, "is a good example: though rebuilt recently, it was constructed in the 1200s."

"Quite," Holmes said. "I'm reminded of the curious case of the Irish rogue with the sinister name, Captain Blood. Late 1600s was it?"

"Why, yes, Mr. Holmes, quite a remarkable story," Walter agreed, offering Holmes a bit of after-dinner candy. "In those days the royal collection was kept in the Martin Tower. The warder charged with their security lived nearby. The fellow, Blood, courted the jewel keeper's daughter, pretending to be a mercenary newly back from the wars. When the time came that he was fully trusted, he brutally struck down the father and, with an accomplice, stuffed his clothing full of sceptres and crowns to carry out of the Tower. He was apprehended, but then pardoned by King Charles for reasons never fully explained. Quite amazing indeed."

"Amazing," Holmes said, "but not unique. Just one of many cases where a criminal first won the hand, then stole the ring, eh Walter?"

The warder turned pale.

"It reminds me of a case," Holmes continued, steepling his long fingers together and tucking his chin as he raised his eyebrows. "Not quite as far back in time as Captain Blood. In fact, it was the first year of your wardership, was it not?"

"Yes, but it could never happen again," Gladstone replied quickly, trying to change the subject. "The Tower only rarely holds prisoners at all now and they of a political nature, not common ruffians."

"I realize that," Holmes admitted. "But was that not a most extraordinary case? What were the particulars again?"

Gladstone hung his head as if in shame or deep thought. His wife reached over and patted his hand, giving it a gentle squeeze.

"Come now, Walter," Holmes said. "This will not do. Not do at all. Perhaps I should offer such details as I already know and you correct me if I stray from the truth. I am thinking of the time that Jonathan Mandon faked an attempt on Queen Victoria's life and received a term in here, awaiting trial."

Walter took over telling the story, slowly and mechanically, as if the words were being drawn from him by great force. "He had a visitor, though he was not supposed to. But it seemed harmless to admit his fiancée for a brief stay."

Holmes nodded his understanding, but when Gladstone seemed reluctant to proceed, Holmes took up the narrative again. "With a hairpin left him by his lady, Jonathan escaped from his cell, heading not for freedom . . ."

"But to the Jewel House," Gladstone concluded. "Yes, it was all a fraud, perpetrated by that scoundrel. The romantic involvement, the assassination attempt, it was all part of his scheme to be locked up near enough to the gems to carry out his intended theft. But no one could have known at the time!" Gladstone said fiercely. "No one!"

"Calm yourself, Walter," Holmes admonished. Then, abruptly, the detective seemed to change the subject. "Is it true that you have two siblings?"

"Three," Gladstone corrected. "All older: one sister, the oldest; and two older brothers. But my sister has passed on. She's been gone ten years now."

"But not without leaving you a niece, eh Gladstone?" Holmes asked. Walter said nothing. "A niece you were very close to, but she did not take your advice in her choice of a future husband, did she?"

"No," Walter said quietly. "No, she didn't. But it was not her fault . . ."

"So that night," Holmes interrupted, "it wasn't about doing a courtesy for a suspected felon, but rather allowing your niece a favor—one you *supposed* to be innocent."

"Yes, Mr. Holmes," said Walter, straightening his shoulders and looking Holmes squarely in the eye. "And though I don't know how you came by this information, there's nothing you can do to me. That unpleasantness was settled long ago. What business is it of yours to bring it up now?" The round face of the white-haired chief warder reddened with anger.

"No, no! You misunderstand me, sir," Holmes said quickly. "It is not about you at all. I have no doubt but what you have punished yourself much more severely than any tribunal ever would have done. But Mandon was never found, was he? And while fortunately he dropped the gem, the uncut Pilot Ruby, he himself was never apprehended."

Walter was silent. He rubbed his hands together as if washing them over and over.

"Yes, sir," Mary said. "That is correct."

"Well, then," Holmes summarized, "in my mind, that makes him one of the prime suspects for another attempt."

"What? Surely you must be joking, Mr. Holmes," Walter cried. "Everyone believes Jonathan drowned that night."

"I realize that was the common belief, but we must discount no possibilities, lest a mishap occur again. You of all people must see the wisdom of that. You must trust me, Walter. You must trust me enough to keep nothing back, no matter how old or insignificant."

———

Duff, his eyes opened wide and his brows raised up to his hairline, tiptoed as he closed the rooftop door of Lanthorn Tower. Peachy hurried him over to where Danny stood with his hands on the warm, softly orange stones of the parapet. They gazed out over the Thames at the early summer sunset. A breeze swelled out of the east, filling the dark red sails of a black-hulled cargo ship heading up river. Lifted by the wind, the ship glided smoothly between the newly laid footings of Horace Jones's invention called Tower Bridge.

"Going to be a lift bridge," Danny said with certainty to Peachy and Duff as they joined him in looking down at the swirling water. "When ships come, the road will lift, and the ships will go through. Then the halves will tilt together again."

"Blimey! Do you really think it'll work?" Peachy said.

"Why not?" Danny answered.

"Are you glocky? What if it gets stuck, then what'll they do?" Peachy asked skeptically. "Bit dotty, if you ask me."

"But Danny," Duff said, pointing to the edge of the road where a line of cabs, wagons, and double-decker horse-drawn omnibuses turned west onto Lower Thames Street, heading for London Bridge upstream. "Won't the carts fall into the water?"

"No, Duff. They'll just have to wait their turn."

"You can see everything from up here," Peachy said, wanting to interrupt Danny's turn as instructor. He turned around, facing the Tower grounds. "The guards in the courtyard, and the other side of the Tower, even the green where they chopped off everybody's head."

Danny turned to look. "Brilliant," he agreed, half-mocking and half in genuine admiration.

"Uhhh," Duff groaned, waving his arms while leaning over the edge of the wall. "Look! There's little crushers down there."

Danny and Peachy smiled at each other and walked over to where Duff was standing. Facing the fort's entrance at the Byward Tower, they could see the top of Wakefield Tower where they had escaped the tour.

"How come they're so little, Danny?" Duff asked.

"They are proper-sized, Duff," Danny explained. "It's us as is high up. See?"

"Do you granny they are looking for us?" Peachy wondered. " S'pose they counted noses and come up three short?"

"No," Danny reassured them after studying the procession of guards and yeoman warders. "That's the ceremony of the keys. It happens every day. Mr. Holmes told me. Let's go down for a closer look."

"Crikey," Peachy argued, "what if we get caught? If they spot us before we find a proper lurk, then the game is up before it's even started."

"Go on," Danny said. "We'll be quiet as mice and dark as night. Besides, Mr. Holmes told us to watch all the doings. We can't do that if we stay up here all the time. Anyway, they won't catch us," he repeated.

"But what if they do? The other visitors have already left. We're in trouble if they tumble that we're here."

"Then we just ask for the chief warder, like Mr. Holmes told us to," Danny remarked.

"Then you blokes go ahead," Peachy concluded. "I'll keep watch from here. If you are determined to get shackled, it makes sense to split up."

"Okay," Danny agreed. "We'll meet you back up here after dark."

"Not hardly," Peachy said, shaking his red mop of hair. "You'll be wearing a terrier crop when next I see you. Just like all the other mugs in Newgate prison." He grabbed Duff playfully by the forelock to show where the police would start shaving a prisoner's head.

"All right!" Duff shouted.

Danny looked back at Peachy and laughed.

"Danny," Peachy said in a more serious tone. "Be careful."

Duff followed Danny back into the narrow, twisting, torch-lit stairwell. Danny felt his way down the stone-walled passage. The damp rocks were rounded and smooth, while a musty scent lingered in the air. Their feet shuffled quickly from each step to the next, down three flights of stairs and into a round room, empty of furniture, but decorated with rose-colored tapestries, woven with green and gold thread into scenes of knights on horseback hunting boars and stags. Danny and Duff quickly slipped across the planked floor and out the heavy oak door, into the gloaming and its purple sky.

A wide, limestone-paved path led them around the side of the Lanthorn Tower to a cobblestone walk. Turning left through a low arched gate, they arrived at Water Lane.

"Halt!" shouted a voice. "Who goes there?"

Danny and Duff bumped into each other as Danny backed up suddenly just as Duff was hurrying forward. In a moment they figured out that the words of the guard had not been meant for them. The boys stacked their heads one on top of the other behind a low wall of the Inner Ward. Cautiously, they peered around the corner to spy out the way ahead.

"Halt," demanded a yeoman warder again. "Who goes there?" he repeated.

"The keys," replied another guard, jingling a dog collar–sized brass ring full of keys as he marched down Water Lane toward the gate in the Bloody Tower.

A fly began to circle Duff's head. Annoyed, he shooed it away.

"Whose keys?"

"Queen Victoria's keys," answered the guard.

The yeoman warder on sentry stamped his feet together loudly, saluted and said, "Pass, Queen Victoria's keys."

The man with the keys turned to face the dark overhang of the Bloody Tower and was escorted by a party of soldiers through the arch and up toward the barracks.

Danny and Duff stood hardly breathing, as if closely watching such a ceremony without permission might be grounds for hanging if they were caught.

The fly returned to Duff's left ear. Distracted, he followed it with his eyes until it landed on a stone in front of him. Raising his hand slowly to shoulder height, he swatted it, squashing it flat.

Danny jumped and swung around sharply to see what Duff had done. "Shh!" he said urgently.

"A fly," Duff said, smiling at Danny as he slowly pulled his hand from the wall. Proudly he showed Danny the squashed insect in the middle of a row of chalk marks.

"Cripes," Danny said, cringing from the black mess. Then he took a closer look at the dusty marks on the wall. There on the smooth limestone of a single cut block were small square shapes. Some had openings on one side and others had dots in the centers. Each was about the size of his pinky nail. "Duff, look at this," he said curiously.

Duff leaned closer. "I know, Danny," he said with pride. "It's the fly I squished."

"Not the fly!" Danny insisted. "I mean these marks. Looks like some kind of writing."

"Writing?" Duff said doubtfully. "I couldn't never read no writing like that."

"I know, Duff. I think it's a code," Danny said, his excitement rising. Here was something to report to Mr. Holmes!

Danny reached in the pocket of his trousers and pulled out his pack of tools and things. From it he removed a small piece of hard charcoal wrapped in a torn scrap of newspaper. Studying the wall, Danny began to copy down the characters. It looked like this:

Concentrating on the writing, Danny and Duff failed to notice as footsteps approached from behind them. "Here now! What are you lads doing in here after closing?" an angry voice demanded.

Frightened and startled, the two boys spun around to face the man. It was a yeoman warder. He had piercing black eyes below coal-black hair, and a sharply pointed hawk's beak of a nose.

He stepped between Danny and Duff and brushed the chalk scratches off with a swipe of his bony hand. "And vandalizing the queen's property, too. Where are your parents? What other mischief have you been about?"

"But sir," Danny replied. "We just found . . ." Then he stopped himself as he recalled Sherlock Holmes's instructions not to trust anyone.

The guard did not seem to notice the abrupt halt of Danny's explanation. "I know what you were doing, lurking about after closing! You'll come with me!"

"Yes, sir," Danny answered, relieved that he had not said more.

Duff walked along eagerly enough, as if it were all

a game. But Danny risked one more glance upward at the Lanthorn Tower where Peachy was hiding. He caught a glimpse of the top of Peachy's head as the third spy ducked down. Danny nodded to himself with satisfaction as he and Duff were escorted through the gate and up the lane, as darkness fell over the land.

FOUR

THE CONVERSATION in the parlor of the Gladstone house had turned to more pleasant things when there was a disrupting knock at the door. "Mary," Walter Gladstone said, "go and see who it is, will you?" She walked down the stairs to the door while Holmes and the chief warder continued their discussion.

"Really, Mr. Holmes," Walter said, "how on earth could you deduce that I was stationed in the Orient at any time? Have you been asking questions about me behind my back?"

"Not at all! It's quite elementary, Gladstone! The use of certain uncommon spices in the excellent meal indicated that you may have been in the Far East. You, yourself, confirmed this possibility by offering me candied ginger as a sweet. Surely such an unusual after-dinner treat is an acquired taste best developed by a military posting of some duration. That observation, together with a certain unusual skin tone that suggests that you have suffered from a fever specific to . . ." Holmes was cut short by the sound of young voices clamoring to see the chief warder.

"What on earth?" Walter exclaimed as the dark-haired, scowling guard reached the top of the stairs with his two youthful prisoners in tow. Danny's eyes lit up when he saw Holmes and he started to speak, but a small signal from the detective made him hold his tongue.

"I caught these brats lurking about after curfew and scribbling on our walls," the warder said. "Seems they stayed behind in the Tower after a Jewel House showing. This big chap here hasn't said much, but the other one does enough talking for two. He requested, nay, that's not right! He *demanded* to see you!"

Holmes tried to suppress a smile. "Chief Gladstone," he said, "would you be so kind as to allow me a word with you in private? I assure you it will not hurt anything to allow these two desperate characters to sit upon your sofa." At another sign from Holmes, Danny and Duff sat down abruptly.

Gladstone looked confused, but agreed. "Mr. Holmes, this is George Fenton, raven master of the Tower. That's fine, George," Walter said. "Wait outside please, until I sort through this mess."

"Aye," Fenton said grudgingly as he turned back toward the stairs. He gave the boys one more glaring look before departing.

"Now, Mr. Holmes," Walter said, "what's all this about, then? Do you know these two? Why did you have me dismiss George?"

Holmes held up a cautioning finger to stem the flow of questions. "Here is a brief explanation that should resolve your concerns. You see, these are my assistants. I instructed them to join the Jewel House tour and then conceal themselves at an opportune moment. They waited until nightfall, then began to roam the grounds, examining the guard posts and gates. Wiggins and Bernard here are part of my test of your security. So if you don't mind, I'll excuse myself and take these gentlemen home."

Gladstone first looked relieved and then smiled broadly as if he had scored a victory over the private detective. "Mr. Holmes," he said, "I can understand the reasoning behind this scheme, but now it has failed. I hope this proves to you that our protective arrangements are complete."

"Oh it has, Mr. Gladstone, it has," Holmes said as he winked at Danny. Danny slyly returned the wink, knowing that Peachy was still undetected.

With that, Holmes cautioned Chief Gladstone and his wife to say nothing to anyone about the detective's involvement with the boys. "The less said, the better," he warned.

"Of course, if you wish it," Gladstone agreed. He seemed to think that Holmes was embarrassed at the failure of the plan and wanted no one to know that the test had been so easily overcome. Holmes excused himself and escorted Danny and Duff out of the house.

Outside the Constable Tower, Danny stopped Holmes and in a whisper told him about the strange chalk markings. "What do you think it means?" Danny asked. "Is it important?"

Holmes looked thoughtful. "There is no way to tell without further study, Wiggins," Holmes whispered back. "Can you recreate it for me?" Danny shook his head and Holmes could only shrug.

———

A thick, swirling fog rolled in with London's fickle summer weather. A steamer, chugging its way upriver, made a rhythmic hammering noise that echoed off the battlements. The steamer's whistle sounded and, floating on the wind, moaned as it swept past the top of the Lanthorn Tower. Peachy sat curled up in a ball against the wall of the parapet. The hair on the back of his neck prickled. When he had been with Danny and Duff, hiding in the Tower overnight had seemed a lark, an adventure. But now, alone in the dark, surrounded by half-seen shapes in the mist and unfamiliar noises, the joy had been replaced by a growing uneasiness.

The door to the roof creaked, as if someone were opening it. Peachy scurried around behind the small brick structure that housed the stairs. He paused a long while listening, but heard nothing further, except the mournful cry of the steamer now far away.

Peachy waited another minute, then stepped out of his hiding place when the door swung wide open, crashing into the frame before bouncing back shut again. He scrambled for concealment, lost his footing on the slate of the roof and fell flat. He squeezed his eyes shut tight, expecting at any moment for someone . . . or something . . . to grab him.

"I don't believe in ghosts," he whispered to himself. "I don't believe in ghosts."

The last shrill cry of the steamboat reached him, and then all was quiet. Upriver, at the Houses of Parliament, Big Ben began to chime in its deep, resonant voice. Then the air all around was filled with the sound of church bells having their once-an-hour conversation. From the musical bells of St. Savior's Church across the river, to the thin pinging coming from St. George in the east, the discord swelled like an alarm or a warning.

"Three," Peachy counted to himself, ignoring all

but the deliberate strokes from Big Ben. "Four . . . five . . . six . . . seven . . . ," he counted aloud. "Please stop at eleven, please stop at eleven," he pleaded. It suddenly seemed important not to be on the rooftop at midnight.

"Dong," it rang a tenth time. "Dong," the eleventh.

Peachy held his breath.

"Dong," the twelfth stroke sounded. Silence fell again. Peachy peeked out and, behind him, on the stones just over his head, something scratched and gave a rasping cry.

Peachy screamed and ran for the door. He reached for the latch, pulling it hard twice. It was jammed. The boy thought he could feel icy cold hands on his back and the sensation increased his strength.

After one more jerk, the latch broke loose from its iron frame, sending Peachy tumbling back onto the cold stone roof. He jumped to his feet and sprinted down the dark spiraling staircase.

Around and around he ran. Inside the dark column there was a moaning sound that seemed closer behind him with every step. Peachy fled down three flights before hearing the conversation of a pair of guards coming up the stairs.

"Give us a hand with the torch, then," a voice said from around a bend not far below where Peachy skidded to a halt.

" 'Old your 'orses, mate. I've got to light it, 'aven't I?" the other replied.

Peachy tried to think of what to do. Spotting an alcove that narrowed to a slit, he tucked himself into the opening. The orange glow of a torch crept up the stairs as the men rounded the corner. Tightly squeezed between the walls built six centuries earlier through which archers could shoot their crossbows, Peachy waited with his fingers crossed. He told himself that if he were to be caught, he would rather it be by the men than a ghost anyhow. Inches from his arm the men passed, deep in conversation, completely unaware of his presence.

"I told you that door was not closed," one warder said as the men neared the top. " 'Ere it is, flappin' in the breeze, like, and us liable to be put on charges for leavin' it so."

"Aye," agreed the other. "There's somethin' uncanny about this old pile. When the bottom door opens, it sucks the top closed, if it's not bolted."

Peachy jumped from the windowsill just as he heard the rooftop panel slam. On the run again, he sprinted down the remaining stairs and out into the courtyard.

———

Having finished the business at the Tower too late to return to their home at Waterloo Road Ragged School, Holmes suggested that Danny and Duff stay the night at Baker Street. Danny readily agreed, especially since he could imagine the reaction of Headmaster Ingram should the boys return without Peachy.

But while Duff slept soundly and snored loudly on the sofa in the parlor, Danny lay awake curled in a chair, thinking about Peachy all alone in the Tower. "Thank goodness it's a warm night," he murmured aloud as he turned over. Just then the house was shaken by the sound of the knocker at the front door. Duff sat straight up and called for Danny. "Ta, Duffer," Danny soothed. "I'm here, it's just someone at the door." Duff lay back down as the sounds of Mrs. Hudson stumbling around downstairs echoed up through the floor.

The knocker sounded again, more insistently this time. Mrs. Hudson yelled, "I'm coming! No need to wake everyone!" Danny heard the door open, but could not distinguish the conversation that followed. Then he heard Mrs. Hudson walk up the stairs past the parlor and up the next flight to Mr. Holmes's room to inform him of the visitor. "Wake up, Mr. Holmes!" Danny heard Mrs. Hudson shout. "You've a visitor!"

"Blimey," Danny muttered. "Mr. Holmes slept through all that blooming racket?"

The parlor door opened and Mrs. Hudson came in. "Daniel," she called softly, "wake up."

"I am already," Danny replied, throwing off the afghan he was wrapped in. "What is it?"

"Mr. Holmes has been summoned most urgently and has requested that you be awakened and told. I cannot imagine what he is thinking to rouse you so."

"It's all right, ma'am," Danny said, uncurling and standing up from the chair. He was instantly concerned that something had happened to Peachy. "Does he want Duff, too?" When Mrs. Hudson gave a negative shake of her head, Danny spared a glance for his friend and found Duff snoring.

Holmes met Danny at the parlor door and they descended the stairs together. The messenger waiting in the entry hall was a yeoman warder. Holmes remarked to Danny that the officer brought a message directly from Chief Warder Gladstone.

"He says it's an emergency, sir," the warder repeated. "He requests that you come at once." Now Danny was really frightened. The alarm must concern Peachy. What if someone had mistaken him for a genuine intruder and done something worse than capture him?

"Chin up, Wiggins," Holmes encouraged, interrupting Danny's thoughts. "I realized that this rude awakening would cause you worry about Carnehan, but don't be concerned. No one would think to send for me in the middle of the night if it was about him. No, this matter is something else entirely. Go back to sleep. I'll return soon." Holmes entered the carriage that waited outside and sped off toward the Tower, while Danny returned to the parlor and tried, unsuccessfully, to fall asleep.

———

"Mr. Holmes!" Walter Gladstone met the detective at the guarded night portal through the Byward Tower. "I'm so relieved you're here."

"What is it, Gladstone?" Holmes asked. "What's so urgent as to require my attendance in the middle of the night?"

"Mr. Holmes, it's about the jewels," Gladstone said in a hoarse, anxious tone. "The Jubilee gifts, I mean. Those jewels!"

Holmes held up his right hand in a gesture demanding silence. "Who else knows of this?" the detective asked in a whisper.

"No one, sir. Why?"

"If there has already been a mishap with the gifts, then anyone here could be involved. Let's go to the storeroom where we can discuss the particulars without fear of being overheard."

The two men headed across the courtyard to the Great Hall of the White Tower where Chief Warder Gladstone explained. "After your little test of our defenses, I thought it wise to personally check the gift storage once more before retiring. While I was studying one of the pieces, supposedly an uncut gem from Sarawak, I accidentally dropped it. Mr. Holmes, it shattered on the flagstone like glass. In fact, it is glass. See, here are the fragments."

"Most interesting," Holmes said, peering closely at the clever fake now cracked in two. "Go on."

"I realized," Gladstone continued, "that it was a forgery, but I assumed that it was intentional and brought that way. You know, the Sultan of Sarawak is anxious to curry favor with Her Majesty, but he may not be able to afford a gift of the highest value. In any case, I intended to take up the matter privately with the Sultan's representative, in order to avoid an embarrassing diplomatic incident."

"But you've come to a different conclusion since?" Holmes asked, his eyes darting around the Great Hall.

Gladstone nodded sadly. "As I tossed the pieces of the fake in my hand, a horrible suspicion crossed my mind: what if there were more fakes than one? So I examined a golden platter. Its weight did not feel exactly right to me. Do you see this tiny mark?" Gladstone pointed to a scratch on the back of the plate. The edges of the scrape were bright gold, but the groove was dull gray. "I did that with my pocket knife. Then I sent for you."

Holmes whipped a large, circular magnifying glass out of the pocket of his overcoat. Through the lens he carefully studied the scratch. "You are quite correct," he announced. "This is lead, thinly plated with gold. Is there more?"

"Indeed, Mr. Holmes! That is the worst of it. I can hardly imagine one nation presenting a forgery as a gift, but I have found five fraudulent pieces, all from different countries! It's a conspiracy, Mr. Holmes."

Holmes wrinkled his eyebrows and looked slightly amused. "A conspiracy by whom and for what purpose?" he asked.

"Why, the Irish Nationalists," Gladstone said with assurance. "Those who want Ireland to be free of Great Britain would like nothing better than to provoke the worst kind of scandal and shame Her Majesty's government."

"Possibly," Holmes agreed, "but this is more likely an ingenious case of theft and substitution so as not to be detected. And that would point to an inside man. Not politics, Gladstone, simply greed."

"Well then, Mr. Holmes, we'll question everyone who has been in the storeroom. Noble or common, English or foreigner, we'll find the culprit, if we have to shake it out of him."

"You forget," said the detective with a cautioning tone, "that many who have been in and out of this room unattended are princes and representatives of kings and other foreign diplomats. To attempt to wrest the truth from them would cause the very scandal you must avoid!"

The chief warder looked almost frantically worried. "But what *can* we do then? This is tragic, terrible."

"It is even worse than you imagine," Holmes said with pity. "If the criminals do not attempt to take more of the gifts, then they have already departed and all is lost."

Gladstone was practically spinning as the depth of the misfortune sunk in. "Then at least we'll post round-the-clock guards here," he said, eager to come up with something to be done.

"No, no!" Holmes warned. "That is exactly what you must not do! There must be no change of routine; no indication that the substitution has been discovered. That is your only hope."

"But how do you know that this crime involves someone who has access to this room? Could it not be a sneak thief?"

The private investigator did not remind Gladstone that only hours before, the chief warder had been boasting of how impossible it was for anyone to sneak about within the Tower. Holmes merely looked up at the iron grates across the high windows and at the key in Gladstone's hand that unlocked the single way in or out of the room.

"So what *shall* we do?" Gladstone said again. He was almost begging now.

"We wait," Holmes said. "We must discover, if we can, all parties to the crime. Then we set a trap to catch them all at once. Therefore, you must not tell another soul, and no deviation from your natural routine should be made. If the criminals catch wind of any abnormal activity, they will escape. In any case, they must believe it is safe to continue their scheme long enough for me to find out who's behind it all. Have courage," Holmes said, clapping the warder on the shoulder. "At this moment, we have the advantage in that the criminals still think themselves to be safe and undetected. I must be off. Go to bed, Gladstone, and remember: say nothing to anyone."

———

Peachy Carnehan, far from being captured by the Tower guards, actually was lying cuddled against the cold stone of the base of the Lanthorn Tower. Warders patrolled the paths on each side of him, one leading past the Wakefield Tower where the crown jewels were kept, and the other tracing the outline of the ancient Roman city wall on its way by the gloomy bulk of the White Tower.

Counting the echoing steps, Peachy could hear but not see the progress of a yeoman warder walking fifty paces up the east walk. The sentry finally stopped at the foot of the White Tower before measuring fifty paces back. Another guard had a similar pattern along the south wall. One was always coming toward Peachy's location when the other was going away. It made it very hard for Peachy to move anywhere, or even to change positions to ease his aching muscles and stiff joints. Only a thick, knee-high fog provided cover for his observations.

Peachy looked around. As long as he stayed low, he was safe from the guards. But who knew what creatures might be hiding out in that fog, or what ghosts for that matter? In some ways Peachy was grateful for the patrolling sentries: their steady tread kept him from being absolutely terrified.

Eight-times-fifty paces Peachy counted and then he began to doze off to the metallic tapping of the guards' shoes striking the pavement. His head drooped to the ground, and the damp gravel pressing into his cheek woke him. He shook his head groggily, and in a half-dreaming state just as his eyes were about to shut again, he saw a kind of tunnel through the fog, as if he were at one end of a long, gray tube. The other end of the mist-walled cylinder stretched away in the darkness, up to Tower Green, the place where queens and others had been beheaded. Peachy's heart raced and his body felt as if it had just been dumped into an ice-cold bath.

Sitting up and scooting backward until his spine scrunched painfully against jutting edges of stone, Peachy thought he was wide awake and yet hoped he was asleep and dreaming. At the far end of the tube and coming directly toward him, a dark shape sliced the fog into swirls and eddies like a great shark parting seawater with its huge dorsal fin.

Peachy's thoughts carried on a terrified babble. *It's the ghost of Anne Boleyn,* he thought. *She's flying across the ground, and she wants to kill me!*

The shape drew closer and closer. Peachy could not clearly make out its form, but there seemed to be a black stump where the head should have been. Peachy's right hand scrabbled along the base of the wall, hunting for a loose stone with which to defend himself.

Faster the shape flew, until it was only feet from him. In all his fear Peachy stood up to fight, swinging the lump of rock with all his strength. The black form swooped over his head, squawking loudly, as if it were offended, before soaring away up the battlements.

Just a blooming raven, Peachy thought. He sighed deeply and, despite the chill he felt, a bead of sweat rolled down his cheek. He imagined that he had frightened the bird as much as it had scared him. "Thank you, God," Peachy murmured, ashamed but nevertheless relieved. He dropped the rock with a clatter, forgetting the nearness of the sentries.

The eastward patrolling yeoman warder stopped in mid-stride, slapping the stock of his rifle as he swung it to readiness. He scanned the territory. Peachy sank back down into the shadows.

"Oy, Graham," the sentry called to the other guard. "Did you hear that?"

"Hear what, mate?" Graham replied.

"That noise. Like someone dropped something."

"Give over, Rodney," the second guard returned in an exasperated tone. "You'll not do that to me again. Trying to give me the williwaws."

"Crikey! I'm not having you on. I know I heard something," Rodney insisted.

Graham stamped the butt of his gun on his boot top. "This shift is bad enough, without you trying to play me for a fool."

Peachy snickered to himself at the thought that he was the cause of their fear.

"Do your job and leave me alone," Graham snapped, and began walking his post again.

Peachy watched as Rodney rubbed his eyes and shook his head before returning to his pattern of fifty paces up and back.

Peachy grinned to himself as a mischievous thought struck him. He decided he could not resist the opportunity.

As Rodney approached his turnaround point, way up the gravel path near some antique cannons, Peachy cupped his hand over his mouth. Turning his head to the side Peachy called, "Graaahaam," in as spooky a voice as he could produce.

"What is it now?" Graham yelled, turning around, expecting to see Rodney right next to him. "Uhhh," he grunted. "Did you call me, Rodney?"

"What?" Rodney asked. "What do you want?"

"I said, did you call me again?" Graham repeated.

"Nay," Rodney answered. "I didn't say a blasted thing."

Peachy placed his hands over his mouth to hold back the laughter. The two guards began to bicker. Peachy pressed his arms close to his sides and huddled back in the shadows when he saw a third tall figure approaching.

"Leave off the chatter you two," a commanding voice ordered. "I can hear you all the way up at garrison."

"Aye, sir, Captain, sir." The two sentries stopped their arguing and snapped to attention with a click of boot heels.

"In any case, I'm to relieve you, so off you go," the newcomer commanded.

"Both of us, sir?" Warder Graham asked.

"Yes, both of you," the officer answered angrily. "Now cut along sharp-like, and no mucking about."

Without another word out of them, Peachy saw Graham and Rodney march up toward the barracks. When they were gone, the unnamed new guard turned south and headed for the Outer Ward, passing within a few feet of Peachy and under the archway of the Bloody Tower. He was gone for several minutes before returning to the path that he patrolled. Peachy listened to the clicking of his boots, then heard a new noise that sounded as if it came from the other side of the inner wall. It was a sound between a splash and a hiss. The guard stopped momentarily in his tracks, then walked briskly away from the disturbance and up toward the White Tower.

Alone at last and finally able to move, Peachy rose unsteadily to his feet and tiptoed over to the edge of the Bloody Tower's arch. The boy leaned slowly around the corner to peer through the opening that looked toward Water Lane. At first he saw nothing at all except torchlight reflecting on the damp stones of Traitors' Gate. Then, just in front of him, there it was. The thing he had heard, the splashing and hissing noise, was caused by the apparition right ahead of him. A giant, rat-like creature, complete with pointed nose and curling tail, was walking down the steps of Traitors' Gate. It never even paused at the edge, but slunk down into the water.

In another moment of terror-inspired strength, one of several the night had already presented, Peachy jumped to reach the grill of the portcullis hanging above him. Climbing the cold iron of the frame as a ladder, he slipped through the narrow slot in the ceiling. Peachy retreated, shivering, to the darkness at the top of the spiked dropgate just as the last of the creature disappeared into the murky water of the Thames.

FIVE

THE DAY FOLLOWING all the adventures inside the Tower of London found the Baker Street Brigade once again at their regular occupation: selling newspapers.

"Extra, extra, read all about it," Danny pitched to the passersby on Minories Street, at the top of Tower Hill. "Dignitaries bring priceless treasures to Victoria for Golden Jubilee celebration. A tanner, a bender, only a sixpence. Read all about it."

"I'll take one of those, my man," said an old fellow dressed in stovepipe trousers and a cutaway coat, a style of the 1850s. He accepted a paper from Danny, handing him coins totaling seven pence. "Keep the odd penny," he said.

"Thank you, sir," Danny said, giving the man his copy of *The Illustrated London News*.

The man picked up the paper, stopping long enough to examine the woodblock print illustration of a teenage Queen Victoria at her coronation some fifty years before. "I remember it like it was yesterday," the old man said, showing Danny the engraving.

On the other side of the street, Peachy called, "Papers, morning papers! Get the news while the print is still warm!"

Duff stood next to Peachy on the corner, holding the papers. A gentleman walked up to Peachy, taking one off his stack. "Cheers," Peachy said, pocketing the change.

"What was it like in there last night, Peachy?" Duff asked politely.

"Cor, Duff," Peachy boasted, "you wouldn't believe it if I told you."

"But did ya see some of them ghosts that guy was talking about, Peachy?"

"I sure did," Peachy said. He bared his teeth and made a scary face at Duff. "Worse than anything you ever saw! Turn your blood to ice, they would."

Duff stepped forward, dropping his head and looking closely at Peachy's eyes. "Was you scared, Peachy? Did ya cry?"

"Naw! I just jumped up and told them leave off their moaning and get outta there," Peachy bragged.

"Wizard," Duff said with admiration. "You must be powerful brave."

Peachy grinned, and nodded his head. At that instant an omnibus went by and clanged its bell for the pedestrians to clear the road. Peachy jumped straight up, almost into Duff's arms.

Sherlock Holmes alighted from a growler, a four-wheeled coach, and collected Danny from the corner before crossing to Peachy and Duff.

"Good morning, gentlemen," Holmes said. "And congratulations, Carnehan, for eluding the pursuit. How did you manage it?"

"I stayed on top of the big spiky gate thing till

morning," Peachy explained. "Then I waited till the first tour of the day come through. When they passed the Bloody Tower, I climbed down and joined the group. When they come out, so did I. Piece a cake."

"And did you have a chance to do any investigating as well as hiding?" the detective asked.

"Oh yes, Mr. Holmes. Indeed, I did. I was almost caught by the guards twice or maybe three times. I was just telling Duff how I seen this big flying thing swooping down on me, only it was a raven," Peachy answered, excited.

A smirk spread across the detective's face. "Really, Peachy."

"Too right! And when I looked about the splashing noise, I seen a giant rat getting into the water!"

"That will do, Carnehan," Holmes insisted. "It's easy to see you have some story conjuring in that redheaded little Irish skull of yours."

"But sir, I ain't fooling," Peachy argued.

"Enough stories for one day! How can I count on you if you let your imagination run away with your good sense?" Holmes scolded.

Peachy, embarrassed and disappointed, stared at the ground, momentarily sulking.

Holmes continued, "Life is a search for truth, not a quest for fairy tales. Anyway, I have some important business for the Brigade. Now listen carefully. There's been a crime in the Tower, and I need you three to go down to waterfront and check out the grog shops and gambling dens for me."

Danny stepped closer. "What are we looking for, Mr. Holmes?"

Raising one eyebrow, and squinting down at his young assistants, the detective said, "You are looking for a soldier. I do not yet know his name, but he's one of the guards in the Tower. I suspect he is quite a gambler, and he may be a drinker as well."

"Crikey," Peachy exploded, "that cuts a wide swath! How many soldiers don't get after drinking and gambling some way?"

"You are correct, Carnehan," Holmes said, not at all angered by Peachy's outburst. "But this man, whoever he is, will be in the company of either a rough crowd or some foreigners or both. Not those with whom you would expect an officer in Her Majesty's forces to associate. Now, finish with your papers and go. I'll find you and hear your report tomorrow," he concluded.

Holmes turned quickly and began to walk off.

"Hold on a jiffy," Peachy insisted. "If this bloke is up to no good, he won't waltz about in his uniform, will he? How are we to know if he's an officer?"

"Observation," Holmes called back over his shoulder, just before disappearing into the crowd on Tower Hill. "Look for polished boots. He won't think to change his footgear." Then he was gone.

"I wonder what this is all about?" Peachy said. "He didn't even tell us what the turn was, or what had been snaffled. And him not letting me finish my tale."

Confused but determined to complete their important task, the Baker Street Brigade set off to the waterfront to look for the mysterious soldier.

———

As soon as the day's supply of papers had been sold, Danny, Duff, and Peachy set off to carry out the curious instructions given them by Sherlock Holmes. They spent some time discussing which area of the waterfront should first receive their attention, then decided to begin with Cubitt Town.

Because of the looping course of the river, Cubitt Town was three miles away from the Tower by water, but a walk of only a mile and a half along the highway. Built in the 1850s to provide cheap housing for the laborers working in the docks and shipyards, Cubitt Town sprang up on the east shore of the Isle of Dogs. The area, which was a peninsula and not an island, was known for its opium dens, illegal gambling halls, and rookeries of crime of every description.

"Find a military man in a betting shop," Peachy said, complaining again about the vague instructions. "Cor! Shouldn't be too hard at all! Only place every sailor and soldier with leave and a packet of cash spends his time!"

"Pipe down, Peachy," Danny said. "And start looking. Besides, we're not looking for a sailor. Mr. Holmes said that it's an army chap we're after."

Peachy rolled his eyes. "Out of uniform it's the same thing, you thickheaded . . . Blimey! Never mind."

The streets of Cubitt Town were filled with muck that stunk worse than the river. Once, a London city surveyor's party took markings on levels at various points within the area and found that many of the streets were actually lower than the river level at certain times of the day, which explained the aboveground pooling of liquid waste. But those who were accustomed to the dodgy life style that went with the warrens and alleys appreciated every aspect of Cubitt Town.

The respect for privacy among the criminals who frequented the false-fronted pubs and grog shops would astound anyone from the outside. For the criminals themselves it was common courtesy to ask no questions and carry no tales, a rare and unique favor that they gave to no one else in their lives.

Anyone asking questions there was likely to wind up beaten and dumped in the river or, if lucky, just ignored. Money got answers, but too often for Scotland Yard and the authorities, the answers were lies, the creator of which would disappear again before the mistake was discovered.

"Well," Danny said, "I say we split up and cool the streets for our man. If we act like we're on the beg, nobody'll think twice about it."

"Right, now who has to take Duff?" Peachy said.

Duff glared at him and frowned. "I'll go with Danny," he said. "And don't get crying to help if you need trouble from me! I mean, don't trouble yourself if I help you start crying. No. Danny, what do I mean?"

"It's all right, Duffer," Danny said. "I grannied what you meant."

"Me, too," Peachy chimed in. "Don't get sore, Duff. I was just having you on. Listen, Danny, I'll stay out on the street and keep an eye on things, while you and Duff go into some of these *businesses.* Come back after you've checked out two or three and make sure I'm not dead." Peachy smiled and Danny and Duff turned to go.

Peachy wondered where to begin, finally deciding to walk toward the river's edge. He carefully eyed the passersby as he went, occasionally asking for spare change. Most ignored him or aimed slaps in his direction, which he ducked. One man did give him a single coin, an American penny. "Crikey! Thanks, your lordship!" he scoffed. "That'll help me when I go there

. . . in about thirty years." But the man walked on, not paying attention to the little beggar in the street.

"Good, pay no mind," Peachy said to himself. "That's the way this is supposed to go. Only I think Mr. Holmes must have gone balmy if he thinks this will turn answers to some high-class crime. There's nothing high-class about this place!"

———

The first establishment Danny and Duff tried was closed, or so said the three heavyset blokes outside. "It's out of business and besides, you're too young for what they're selling." Danny laughed at the inconsistency, making Duff smile as well, though he did not understand the humor.

The second building they approached was a run-down dive called The Angel. The worn-out sign once had depicted a wise being with widespread wings and outstretched, welcoming arms, but now the wings were missing and the extended arms looked ready to grab the unwary.

Danny and Duff joined a group of men in striped shirts and dungarees who were just entering the pub. The two boys were admitted with the group as though they were all together. Once inside, Danny motioned for Duff to follow him till they found an unoccupied table where they could sit and watch. "Danny?" Duff said, looking pointedly at each man in the place. "What type of soldier again?"

"An army man, Duff, but don't stare. And don't talk to anyone. Crikey! They all look like rampsmen and buzzers."

Duff lowered his gaze to his feet as he followed right behind Danny through a curtained doorway. The room behind the greasy cloth partition was full of hushed conversation. Small knots of men bent over grimy glasses of brown or clear liquid. It was easy for Danny to imagine that the talk concerned trading money for opium, or dealing in stolen children like the Mahdists did.

The room fell silent as they entered and all eyes turned toward them. Duff looked up, realized that everyone was staring at him and immediately dropped his head again. "What do you want here?" a gruff voice demanded from a booth behind them.

"Not to see you buzzers and rampsmen," Duff blurted. Danny's stomach dropped in fear.

"What's that?" someone else said. "You chavvies having us on or be you noses for the crushers?"

"N-no, sir," Danny said. "No, uh, my father was . . ." He tried to think fast, but no words would come to him. He felt the piercing stare of many suspicion-filled eyes. It was easy to think of their hands fingering blackjacks or sharpened knives. He swallowed hard and tried again. "My father is a sailor, he . . ."

"Oh?" a one-eyed man challenged from directly behind him. "What's his name, then? Maybe I killed him." The top lid of the empty eye socket drooped flat against the man's cheek. "Something wrong, boy?" he asked as he drew a curved-blade sailor's knife. Now standing less than a foot away, Danny could smell the man's foul breath. "Looking at my eye?"

Indeed, Danny realized he was gaping at a large scar that ran from the man's chin up the left side of his face. The whitish gash stopped at the missing eye.

"No, sir!" he said quickly as he looked away.

Danny heard the complaint of chair legs scraping across the floor behind him. Another man said, "I think he was, Lefty. I think he was gawkin' right at that missin' squint of yourn. Mayhap he's seen your perty mug on a Peeler's flyer. That's it!"

The one-eyed man named Lefty put the tip of his blade under Danny's chin and lifted the boy's head up. Danny sensed that the other man had closed off escape from behind. What could they say to get out of this? If he lied, they would know and if he told the truth he would be admitting that they were working for the law. Where was help?

"That true, laddie?" Lefty smiled with blackened and missing teeth. "You can get a closer look while I'm chewing you up and swallowing your miserable little . . ."

"Ah, my boys!" A woman's voice came from a booth at the far back wall. Danny looked up in surprise. "My lovely children come to see Momma at work." The crowd suddenly roared with laughter. She spoke with a slurring accent as she rose from her seat next to a large unshaven man and walked toward them. The woman, whom Danny had never seen before, had dark brown hair and deep blue eyes that shone even in the dimly lit back room. "I told you to go straight home, Dino. What are you doing here?"

Danny and Lefty both looked confused. "Uh," Danny stuttered.

"You are supposed to keep your father company until I return, you naughty boy. Shame on you! Go home at once."

He caught on then and joined the performance. "But Momma," he whined, "Poppa wanted his meal so long ago that he sent me to find you." The crowd laughed and the men stepped away, returning to their drinks.

"Go outside and wait for Momma," the woman instructed.

Danny turned toward the door and with Duff in tow, walked outside. They were out there only a few moments when the woman joined them. "Duff," Danny said softly as his pulse returned to normal, "you can look up now."

The woman drew close to them and looked around before speaking. "Just what are you two doing in a place like this? Don't you know it's dangerous around here for people your size?"

Danny noticed that the woman's slurred speech had suddenly corrected itself. Her words were clipped and direct. He struggled to find an answer. "Yes ma'am, we were just . . ."

"You were just . . . ," she interrupted. "Well don't! Whatever it was you were doing can get you killed. Now if you don't mind, I have to get back in there before they have time to think of questions. You may have just cost me two week's work."

Not at all clear what this meant, Danny said, "Well, why did you do it then? You could've let me brass it out." Duff looked up at last and smiled. He realized that Danny was talking braver now that they were outside the tavern.

"I'm working for the Metropolitan Police," was the woman's startling reply. "I'm here in Cubitt Town to pick up word on translators . . . you know, them as sells stolen goods. I only hope you two didn't queer my pitch. Now I have to explain a couple of kids and a husband nobody ever heard of before! Now get out of here!" With that she gave the two a shove and sent them down an alley away from The Angel.

While Duff and Danny were meeting the crowd in The Angel, Peachy was having an interesting encounter of his own. Tiring of panhandling on the main street, Peachy walked along the dockside shanties where small games of dice and other betting opportunities were offered. Being closer to the water meant a change in the aroma from the odor of the Cubitt Town streets, but it still did not smell nice by any means. Peachy drew scowls from scarred sailors with hoop earrings, one-legged men stumping about on wooden pegs, and old tars missing three fingers. None of these seemed to have any regard for human life, making Peachy wish he had brought Duff with him. Not that Duff would be any form of protection from these frightening forms, but at least, two boys together would be less likely to provoke an attack. Or provide two targets for the price of one, Peachy thought.

"Hey, boy!" a snivelling voice beside him shrilled. "Would ye like ta buy a bit of the truth?" The man sitting on the ground in the shelter of an upturned packing crate had no legs below the knees. He wore smoked-lens glasses and a bushy, unkempt beard. The figure gently rocked back and forth, looking nowhere in particular.

"What was that?" Peachy asked as he bent down.

"I said, would ye like ta buy some information?"

Peachy, remembering the numerous disguises of Sherlock Holmes, could hardly contain himself when he figured out who it was. It was just like Holmes to put them in an investigation and then show up there himself in one of his many well-acted roles.

"Why, yes sir," Peachy said, certain that this was

the correct reply. "I'll take whatever news you may have to sell."

"For just a tuppence lad, I'll tell ye everything I know," crooned the beggar.

Still sure it was Holmes, Peachy reached in his pocket and pulled out a coin. "Here you are sir, speak."

Peachy then leaned closer, positive that he had performed his part of the charade; now the detective would give out some new secret instructions.

But the figure sang,

> In waters, mound or underground,
> By surface or by air;
> The mist will still the whippoorwill,
> A devotion he will swear.
> Before the dawn becomes a song,
> A raven there will be;
> And for the top a small rain drop,
> Which still he roams to sea.

"Crikey! What's the point of that, Mr. Holmes?" Peachy said. "Is it a code?" Then the man rolled over, proving without doubt that he really had no legs below the knee. Peachy turned pale and began walking rapidly away.

"Wait, boy," the beggar called after him. "For another tuppence, I can tell ye everything *you* know, too!" He cackled a laugh that sent chills up Peachy's spine.

The boy hurried on along the water's edge until there were no more people to see; no gamblers, no sailors, and no more crazy old men without legs. "Blimey!" he scolded himself. "Why do I do it? Can't tell a ream almsman from a detective? Where's your head, Peachy Carnehan?" Peachy's self-accusation was interrupted when he heard two hissing voices near some large cargo containers. He suddenly remembered the mission he was supposed to be on before he got side-tracked and scooted up next to a canvas-covered shed to listen.

"I said that's impossible," one voice said. "We'll have no more money to pay you if we don't continue to move them."

"If I don't get more money, I can stop this whole thing right now."

"Oh, and how wise of you would that be? How could you possibly explain to your chief? Do you think you'll turn nose on me now? By the time the words were out of your mouth, we'd be back in our own country, and you'd be twisting in the wind. You are only the raven in this scheme, but you stand to take the fall for it all. Do you want that?" Peachy heard no answer. "Good!" the second voice continued. "Then do as I say and everything will be fine."

"I must get back. If I'm gone too long they'll wonder."

"Then go, and put that cape back on!" The flow of words stopped then.

Peachy heard footsteps coming his way, circling the tarp. He sat down quickly and tucked himself under a corner of the canvas. A man stepped right next to where Peachy was hidden and paused, looking around for snoops. Peachy stared at a pair of neatly polished military boots. He dared not look up for fear that any motion would direct the man's attention to him and he would surely end up dead. The soldier tore up a bit of paper, dropped it and then walked on.

Peachy waited till the sound of the tread faded, then thinking the scrap of paper might be a clue, he retrieved the bits of trash. Peachy saw that it was the ripped up fragments of a bookie's stub, for a gambling debt; some horse race or other. John Stone, the bookie's name was. The boy stood up and leaned against the boxes, staring at the back of the cloaked man walking away. Peachy willed the figure to turn, to give him a glimpse of the face. For a split second the man did turn his head and Peachy saw part of a cloaked profile.

"Here now!" A hand clenched Peachy by the shirt collar. "How long have you been there?"

Peachy, thinking rapidly, squinted, shrugged, and shook his head. He motioned to his ears with both hands as he had seen deaf people do to show their lack of hearing.

"How long?" the man shouted right in his ear. Peachy tried not to wince at the sharp pain and when the man looked him in the face again he saw that the ruse had worked. The hooded figure pushed Peachy away, aimed a kick at the boy's backside and laughed as Peachy stumbled and ran away.

SIX

THE BUILDING HOUSING the Waterloo Road Ragged School in which the boys lived appeared old and run-down to anyone who did not realize what it stood for. Situated in a converted warehouse, the charity housed, fed, and educated children whose home normally would be the streets of London.

Summer break gave the children who stayed at the school leave to come and go as they pleased, to run and play. Or, as was the case with the Baker Street Brigade, whom Holmes affectionately called the Irregulars, there was more time to work and make as much money as they could before the school term came around again.

The three friends had not yet reported to Sherlock Holmes on their excursion into Cubitt Town. Since early morning they had been selling papers around Parliament Square at a furious pace. Mobs of countryfolk and foreigners were crowding into London in anticipation of the queen's Jubilee ceremony, now only days away. It seemed to Danny that there were five times as many customers for news as ever before.

"Peachy," Danny said with satisfaction, "if we keep hawking papers like this, we'll be the only blooming newsies they need."

"Newsies?" Peachy exclaimed. "We'll own the paper! Oy, Duffer! Hurry it along, I'm hungry!" Peachy called over his shoulder without looking back.

"That's a first," Danny said. "Usually it's Duff tugging us along to the prog."

Duff caught up just then and asked, "When are we eating, Danny?" Peachy and Danny laughed as they walked through the door of the school.

"Ahh, here is my brigade of irregulars at last!" The boys recognized the voice immediately as it echoed inside the bare brick entrance hall. "How glad I am to see you back."

"Mr. Holmes," Peachy said, "yesterday was so glocky! And the day before, alone in that great pile of stones!" Spending a frightening night in the Tower, getting muddled with the beggar who was not really Sherlock Holmes and being caught snooping in Cubitt Town had plainly spoiled Peachy's taste for detective work. "You don't mean to send us back, do you?"

"How can I say, Carnehan, before I hear your report?" Holmes rebuked with a trace of exasperation. "Tell me of yesterday's search."

Peachy sighed and thought about the amount of the story he could tell without being laughed at by the detective. "Well," he slowly began. "Danny and Duff got into a right shindy and had to get bailed out before they got scuppered."

"Not half, Mr. Holmes!" Danny interrupted Peachy's comments. "I'll tell you everything Peachy told us!" Danny turned to his friend and made a face.

Holmes did indeed laugh at the end of the story;

not because of the mistaken identity of the beggar, but because of the way Peachy saved himself. "Splendid!" Holmes chuckled. "It is a good lead, Carnehan. We cannot say if it is our man or not, but with that betting stub, we'll soon follow it up. Congratulations . . . now, here is what I think you must do next."

"Oh, no!" Peachy jumped back a step from Holmes's intimidating gaze. "I'll not be doing anything by myself anymore. Not just me . . ."

"Carnehan?" Holmes raised his voice into a scolding manner. "There will be nothing dangerous about it at this point, I can assure you. And since you saw the man in question . . ."

"Only his nose and the side of his face and nothing of the second man, I swear it!" Peachy protested. "Why can't you send Duff?"

"No, no," Duff argued. "I'm hungry!"

"So?" Peachy insisted, while Holmes tried to regain control. "Blimey! Eat before you go!"

"Here now!" A voice came from down the hall beyond the bickering group. "What's all this ruckus?"

"Master Ingram!" Danny said. "We were just discussing a case with Mr. Holmes here." Ingram strode up to the boys. The headmaster's hair was dark and his features sharp. His stocky and athletic body and quick wit made him a good model for the orphan boys of the school, but most of all they appreciated his willingness to stand up for them.

"Ah, Mr. Holmes," Ingram said, "I did not recognize you."

"Quite all right, headmaster. I enjoy being unrecognizable. It helps in my line of work."

Ingram laughed. "Well," he said, "you boys don't be too long now. Your dinner will get cold and you know how that bothers Duff here. Good-bye, Mr. Holmes."

"Actually, sir," Holmes said, raising his hand to stop Ingram's departure, "two of these gentlemen will again be in my employ this evening, if you have no objection." Holmes pointed to Danny and Peachy.

"Very well, Mr. Holmes. Duff, why don't you come with me to dinner?" The detective nodded good-bye to Duff and the schoolmaster, then turned back to Danny and Peachy. It was clear that his mind had already dismissed the other discussion and was racing toward the next solution.

"Carnehan, my lad," Holmes continued.

"Peachy!" Danny urged. "Listen to Mr. Holmes or he'll find other people to do our job. And then where would we be?"

Peachy was silent after that.

"Now Carnehan," Holmes started again. "Your task is to go back to the Tower." Peachy shuddered, but Holmes pretended not to notice. "Spending the night there will give you the opportunity to identify the man you saw yesterday, if he is among the guards or the warders. You would know him again, would you not?"

Peachy grudgingly admitted that yes, he would be able to pick out the soldier he had glimpsed in Cubitt Town, if he could see the man's profile again.

"Brilliant!" Holmes complimented the boy. "I knew you were clever enough for this work! Chief Warder Gladstone will even be expecting you, and you'll sleep in his house."

"See, Peach?" Danny said. "That's a proper layout and not bad by half."

Peachy glared at him as he spoke. "Right-o," he sighed, "when do I *get* to go?"

"That's the spirit, lad. Just stay here and I'll make arrangements. Remember one thing: talk to no one about your business there! Should you identify the man, remember that he has not seen you and cannot know that you are on to him. Act naturally! You are now Chief Yeoman Warder Walter Gladstone's great-nephew."

"Blimey! But what if it is Gladstone? What if I identify Gladstone himself?" Peachy asked. "I mean I've never seen him either. What if he's the guilty bloke?"

"Not to worry, Carnehan. I do not think your conjecture can be true, but if it is, just stay put. The criminal would not try anything foolish while I'm watching him so closely. Now go upstairs and eat. A carriage will be back to fetch you in an hour or so."

"But Mr. Holmes," Peachy protested, "do you not mean to even tell us what the man has done? I mean, we don't know what we're facing here."

With this position Danny agreed. It was time for the Brigade to be trusted with more information than they had been given so far. He nodded gravely and stood shoulder to shoulder with Peachy.

Holmes considered their request. "All right, boys," he said finally. "I do not want to put you in additional danger, but you have proven yourselves able to keep silence when it is required. I still cannot say exactly what the crime is, but it involves counterfeiting, stealing, and passing stolen goods. It could even be a worldwide scandal if not solved at once."

"Cor!" Peachy puffed. "Knapping, translating, and doing a bit of the soft?"

"Exactly," Holmes agreed. "Just what I said."

Peachy felt like royalty when Chief Warder Gladstone's coach came to Waterloo Road School to pick him up. The black, four-wheeled carriage was drawn by a matched pair of prancing chestnut horses. It had the silhouette of the White Tower, the symbol of the Tower of London, embossed in gold on the doors.

Other children gathered around the school's doorway, pointing and jabbering as the driver opened the door and let down a folding stair to the plush velvet interior. Much to his embarrassment, Peachy was summoned as "Master Peachy Carnehan." The driver did not allow him to pick up his own bag, though it was just a carpet-sided overnight bag. All the children came outside to see the carriage.

When Peachy first stepped onto the pavement, it struck him that the driver could be the criminal! Peachy hung back, shielded by the crowd, and pretended to gawk as they did until he was sure that the old, fat warder driving the carriage was not the one that he had seen the night before. So, having been sent off in style, Peachy made his return to the Tower.

"I could get used to this," Peachy said to himself beneath the clopping sound of the horses' hooves. "Maybe someday I will."

After crossing the river on London Bridge, the coach turned east and started down the bumpy cobblestones of Lower Thames Street to the Tower entrance. At the gate of the Middle Tower, outside the actual walls of the fortress, a guard in a tall, bushy bearskin hat halted the carriage and inspected the inside. The soldier did not say anything, just looked, then stepped away again. Peachy guessed that the salute the guard snapped was for the official carriage and not for himself, but he sat up a little straighter just the same.

Once inside the gate, the wooden panel closed behind them and the carriage came to a halt. It was there that he was met by his "Great-Uncle" Gladstone. "Hello, young Peachy," Gladstone said with an expansive gesture. "I'm so glad to see you. Your great-aunt and I have been waiting so long for this day to come. Step out here and let me take a look at you." Peachy was relieved to notice immediately that Gladstone was not the man he had seen in Cubitt Town.

The freckled boy jumped out of the carriage and looked around at the parapets and the walkways where he had spent the most terrifying night of his life just days before. It still gave him chills. "Come along now!" Gladstone urged. "Your aunt has prepared a nice meal for you. You must be famished after such a long journey."

Peachy smiled to himself as he thought that the truth was somewhat different than the playacting: his journey had been only about twenty minutes long. But he was hungry, right enough, and he played along with the chief warder as they walked up the steps and across the expanse of the fort to the Constable Tower.

When Peachy entered the doorway, he found the place decorated with all sorts of artifacts from different parts of the world: a testament, Peachy assumed, to Gladstone's long and varied career as a soldier. It came to him that Gladstone did not know that he had remained hidden the other night in the Tower. At this moment, Peachy realized he knew more about the actions of Sherlock Holmes than the chief warder did.

Something like that very thought must have entered Gladstone's mind. When the door shut behind him the white-haired warder said, "Now, lad, do you mind telling me what this is all about?"

"I mustn't, sir. Mr. Holmes gave me clear instructions to talk to no one about my business here."

"That's just fine!" Gladstone shouted angrily. "That Holmes has been more trouble than he's worth. First two boys caught lurking about while crimes are taking place, and now he foists another off on me and keeps me lying to my own officers!"

Peachy blushed and looked at the ground.

"Walter!" his wife scolded. "You are making the lad feel unwelcome! Now stop it. After all, it's not his fault what his instructions are from Mr. Holmes. Do you allow your men to question your orders?"

Peachy was grateful for her assistance. He did not know what he could have said to calm down Gladstone without giving away more than Holmes wanted.

Mrs. Gladstone stopped reproving her husband and smiled at Peachy. "Now dear, my name's Mary. Are you hungry? I've cooked a nice roast and baked a fresh pie for later. Come along now." She smiled. "Walter, take the boy's bag upstairs to the guest room."

Peachy followed her into the kitchen where the combined smells of the rich roast beef and cinnamon-spiced pie made his stomach growl. "Oh, you are hungry! Let's dish you up some of this. And I'm sorry about Walter. We never had children and he doesn't know how to handle them."

Just then Gladstone came into the kitchen. He sounded much calmer. "There," he said, "Peachy is all set up. May I eat now also?"

"Of course you may, Walter," Mary said. "I think the cat may have left some milk in its bowl last night. Go and see if it's not dried up yet. You may help yourself." The teasing over, Peachy smiled as she retrieved another plate from the cupboard and began piling food on it for her husband also.

————

While Peachy enjoyed dinner with his newfound "relatives" in the Constable Tower, Sherlock Holmes departed with Danny to return to Cubitt Town.

"You must never allow the people from which the information is to be extracted to know that the information is valuable," the detective said to Danny as the two-wheeled hansom cab clattered along East India Dock Road toward the Isle of Dogs. "The question is, how to make the bookie talk without thinking he is giving anything away. Bookmakers often operate on the knife-edge of the law and they know they would soon lose their trade if word got round that they were sources of information for the authorities."

"If they was turned?" Danny translated into street talk. "Yes, sir, I can see that plain enough." The boy wrinkled his brow in thought before commenting further, "I guess the answer is to pretend you already know what he's telling you."

"Exactly, Wiggins!" Holmes applauded, pleased that Danny had caught on. "If only Inspector Lestrade of Scotland Yard was as apt a pupil! Now tell me: what do we already know about the man in question?"

"He's in the military," Danny said. "And it seems clear he is a gambler if he had a bookie's chit. Is there more?"

"Actually, yes," Holmes replied, ticking off bits of information on his slender fingers. "We know that the fellow is in some debt . . . that he has performed a service for pay and is expected to perform again for more money . . . that he is afraid someone will hear of his activities . . . and that the threat of exposure keeps him in line. Additionally, whoever is behind the threat feels secure in being able to escape prosecution by leaving the country. We even have Peachy's description of the second figure's dress and speech, uncertain though it may be."

The cab came to a halt in front of a shabby wooden building. The structure definitely leaned to one side and it seemed to Danny that only the brick building to the right propped up the other from falling down flat. There was no sign above the door, but badly chipped, painted letters in the flyblown and grimy window read JOHN STONE, WAGGERS. Danny stared for a moment before he realized that the sign did not refer to dogs; the word *wagers* was misspelled. The place looked deserted and no one was in sight.

"Come along, Wiggins," Holmes said, stepping over a mud puddle and striding toward the entrance. "The game is afoot." From inside the dim interior, Danny could hear the rumble of low conversation. It put him uncomfortably in mind of the pub from which he and Duff had narrowly escaped.

No one in the gambling shop paid any attention to them. Around small tables sat men drinking and playing cards while they waited for the arrival of news about the sporting events on which they had wagered.

Holmes was approached by a short, portly man with a bald head, a fringe of gray hair, and grayish stubble on his cheeks. The man waddled when he walked. "Can I be of assistance?" he asked in a friendly enough fashion.

"Is the proprietor in?" Holmes asked. "Delrick Albion is my name."

"At your service," replied the fellow in his too-tight, too-short pants and bulging waistcoat. "Honest John Stone."

"Ah, quite," Holmes acknowledged, withdrawing the torn betting ticket from his inside coat pocket. "I recently sponsored a party for some soldier friends returning from Zululand. After our gathering my servant found this, which I believe is from your establishment." Holmes held the ticket by the middle so that the tear would not show, then whipped it quickly back out of sight.

"Yes, sir," John Stone agreed, "that is my chit."

"Inasmuch as I do not know to which of my guests it belonged, would you be so kind as to listen as I mention a few possibilities so that I may return it to its owner? He may have won a great deal of money."

"Not necessary, sir," the bookmaker replied with a quick bob of his head. "Just give me the number writ there and I'll tell you double-quick whose it is."

"Well of course." Holmes beamed. "How clever of you. The number is 110429."

Bookie John Stone withdrew a clothbound ledger from under a low counter. Wetting a stubby finger on his tongue, he flipped back several pages. "Oh," he said unhappily, "I don't think this will be of much use to you after all. It says here the name is Dingle, but I don't think that's his ream moniker. I remember him now. You're right about him being a soldier chap, but I'm afraid he backed a losing proposition."

"Really?" Holmes said. "How unfortunate. Does he owe you much money?"

Stone shook his head. "Debt's been paid. It was past due, but then a foreign gent, judging by his accent, come in and settled up for Dingle. I recollect one odd thing: one of the gold pieces he give me was Dutch."

"Dutch," Holmes repeated. "Then that must have been Mr. Pearson."

The bookie shrugged. "You'd be knowing about that," he said. "Didn't give his name, just paid up for Dingle. You'll pardon me, sir, if I say I did not ask no questions. The sum owed was quite large and late. I was glad to see the matter cleared up."

"Yes, quite," Holmes agreed. "Thank you for your help, Mr. Stone."

When Holmes and Danny were outside, the detective muttered to himself, sounding agitated. "Who is Dingle? And why a Dutch coin? Is that significant?" Turning to Danny he said, "Well, Wiggins, we seem to have struck a dead end. Let us hope Carnehan is having better luck."

SEVEN

IT OCCURRED TO Peachy that Holmes's instructions were rather vague. How was he supposed to locate the mysterious military man? By going from officer to officer and asking to view each of them in profile? The guilty one would be up to guilty doings, Peachy reasoned, and that meant being out at night. Finding someone acting suspicious, he decided, would be the first step in finding the right man.

After dinner, Peachy pretended exhaustion and went to his room to sleep. When darkness fell, he opened a window and climbed down a lattice outside, emerging on the wall walk that linked the Constable and Broad Arrow towers.

Stepping out into the warm summer evening, Peachy found himself irritated with the change in the weather. He wondered why it couldn't have been like this last night, instead of so creepy and foggy.

He crept along the east side of the square. From his concealment behind the shrubs planted there, he could hear the footsteps of soldiers as they marched along their rounds.

"Crikey," Peachy whispered to himself, "sounds like a bloomin' thousand of 'em." He realized that it was in fact only one man along the wall to the north, his boots echoing loudly against the thick rock walls. Peachy's confidence grew and he thought he could easily slip by one guard.

Moving up to the last shrub in the row, Peachy waited for the guard's return. When the sentry drew near, Peachy searched his face by the flickering torchlight and realized that it was not the man he had seen on the waterfront. As soon as the guard turned to march in the other direction, Peachy rose from his hiding place and followed, walking in time to the rhythmic footfalls. The guard's patrol was long, following a wall that curved to the left.

Peachy walked so far behind that he would, should the guard turn around, be able to drop flat and not be noticed. *This bloke's gone so long in one direction,* Peachy thought, *I could have chiseled through the White Tower before he got back.*

Just then the warder stopped. Almost caught unawares, Peachy flopped quietly to his stomach and lay with his chin on the cobblestones. The man turned slowly around and peered directly over Peachy's location, but did not notice anything amiss. The sentry took a step back toward the boy, looked some more, then walked on.

Peachy realized that the yeoman warders and the other guards patrolled the walls and all around the buildings, but what of the inner courtyard where the ravens perched? There he might be able to move more freely. When the guard had moved enough distance away, Peachy rose from the cobblestones and crept toward the wall of the White Tower. There he walked west toward the grassy area beyond.

In the moonlit summer night, Peachy could make out the huge dark forms of the ravens. They did not stir and all appeared asleep. Peachy crept on. He reasoned that he could sit in the middle of the grassy space near the pens and get a good look at most of the guards as they walked their patrols. Stepping over the low cast-iron rail, in place to keep visitors off the grass, he sat down next to the flock of birds.

One raven awoke and eyed the boy cautiously, but made no sound. So Peachy sat and waited as each guard along the three walls came and went on his rounds. Two of the soldiers held lanterns and Peachy could easily tell that neither was the man he had seen. The third guard carried no light and walked with his head down as he passed each torch on the wall. Peachy would have to get closer to study the man's face. But as he rose to move across the lawn again, first one and then another and then several of the ravens awoke and began squawking.

"No . . . shhh!" Peachy tried to hush them. He then realized that they were not frightened of him; in fact they were running toward him and away from the very same guard who was now coming directly that way. Peachy scrambled backward on his hands and toes, trying to stay low but move quickly at the same time.

Peachy moved so quickly that he ran into the iron rail and hit his forearm on it. He bit his lip and tried to keep from groaning.

The birds kept moving as the guard walked onto the lawn. One bird that did not retreat from the man's approach was kicked and sent squawking a few feet into the air. Peachy was sure that the guard had seen him because he strode, angrily, right in his direction.

The guard stopped in the middle of the lawn. Peachy watched as he reached into his pocket and withdrew a packet of something that he began to throw at the ravens. They screeched as the food pelted them with hurting force.

"Food's here," the man grumbled. "Eat up, little beggars."

The figure walked about, heaving chunks of raw meat at the birds, making them as angry as he sounded himself. When a raven stopped too long in one place, the man booted it as he had done to the one before.

"Well, what have we here?" the raven caretaker grumbled. Peachy was so intent on the actions of the guard, he had forgotten to conceal himself. "Another after-hours case?" Peachy froze as the man bent at the waist and, looking like a fierce raven himself, charged toward the boy. "Or did you come for a beating like I give to the birds?" He growled the last word as he lunged for Peachy.

Peachy shot straight up and ran from the man through the courtyard, all the while picturing his raven-like features, his large pointed nose, dark-colored deep-set eyes, and pitch-black hair. He ran quickly but clumsily and without any sense of where escape could be found.

Heading for the main gate, all Peachy could think was to flee from the haunting image and the yell that the raven master gave to alert the other guards about the intruder. He ran through the gate and turned left on Water Lane.

Peachy was passing Traitors' Gate when his toe caught a protruding cobblestone and he tripped, falling right on both elbows, scraping them badly. He lay there for a moment before rolling over on the steps by the water, hoping the pursuing guards would run past him.

Peachy suddenly realized that he was lying in the exact spot where the rat figure had descended into the river. The thought made him jump up and put the corner of a wall between him and the pool. When he peered around the angle, he did not see a giant rat, but he did notice some peculiar chalk marks, just like those Danny had told him about.

There was a row of boxes and partial boxes, some with dots inside them. It looked like this:

"Remember," Peachy said to himself. Then the raven master found him, grabbing him roughly by the arm already sore from banging against the railing. "Don't hurt me!" Peachy yelled. "My uncle is Walter Gladstone!" The guard let go of him and he fell to the ground again with a thud.

"You little scamp." The raven master scowled. "Shall we go there and see him then?"

"Too right," Peachy said, regaining some of his bluster. "And I'm going to tell him about how you kick the birds and make them mean!"

The man narrowed his eyes as he thought about the prospect of being in trouble with the chief warder. "Here now," the man said, "no harm done is there? What say we just leave off telling anybody?" he finished, just as the other guards ran up. "Pay no mind, men, this is the chief's nephew, out for a bit of a midnight stroll."

One of the other warders recognized Peachy from

having seen him arrive in the coach and confirmed the story. The guards helped the boy to his feet and brushed him off. "But what're you doing out this late at night? This is no place to be lollygagging about."

"I'm just exploring," Peachy said, trying to sound innocent. "Look, you don't tell my uncle I came out and I'll go right to bed, I promise!"

"What's in it for us, then?" one of the guards joked.

"I'll tell you what." Peachy stopped sounding innocent. "Aren't you the bloke on the west wall? I saw you sipping from that flask inside your coat." The man stopped smiling. "And you!" Peachy gestured toward the other. "You don't even walk your rounds. All you do is sit and smoke. Now believe me, mates, I've seen it all tonight and if you know what's good for you, you'll go on about your business!" There was some grumbling about cutting Peachy up and feeding *him* to the ravens, but the men filed quickly away, back to their posts and rounds and duties.

———

"Danny," Duff called softly from his cot.

"What is it, Duffer?" Danny replied sleepily.

"Do you think Peachy is all right?"

"Sure," Danny said. "How much trouble can he get in when he's staying at the chief warder's house?"

Duff seemed satisfied with this answer; at least he was quiet for a time. Then, just as Danny was drifting off again, he asked, "What's gen-u-ine mean?"

"What?"

"I heard you and Peachy talking about what Mr. Holmes said . . . somebody doing a bit of the soft,

Peachy said. Counterfeit, Mr. Holmes said. Fakes and genuine. What's it all mean?"

Danny, now fully awake, but anxious to satisfy Duff so that he could get back to slumber, did his best to answer. "Fake is when something isn't real . . . genuine is real."

"Oh," Duff said. "Like what?"

Patience wearing thin, Danny continued, "Fake money is called counterfeit. Or there can be fake jewels, like made out of glass, or fake gold, like painted."

"Oh," Duff said.

There was silence for a period of time, but Danny was too well acquainted with Duff to believe the question machine had run down already. So when Duff cleared his throat, Danny said, "Yes, Duff?"

And as if there had been no break in the conversation, Duff inquired, "Why does it matter? I mean, if it looks pretty, like the real stuff, why do people care if they have fakes or gen . . . gen . . ."

"Genuine," Danny concluded. "It's because genuine also costs more, or is harder to get, or means more to someone who has it. Genuine means valuable. Fakes don't."

Silence again, then: "Danny, do people come as fake or genuine, too?"

Now it was Danny's turn to be silent and thoughtful. He had certainly met genuine people: Mr. Holmes, for one, Headmaster Ingram for another, Peachy. He had also met the other kind: kids who only wanted to be friends for what they could get out of you. And somewhere in the Tower, if Mr. Holmes was right, there was a man who looked like a real guard, on duty, protecting things, but was really a dangerous criminal himself.

"Yes," Danny replied at last. "People do come both ways. Some are genuine and some are fake. Sometimes what blokes tell you and what they do are different things; those are the fakes. The genuine ones always do what they say they will do."

"How does a bloke get to be genuine, Danny?"

"I think you ask God, and he helps you with it, mate."

"I want to be genuine always," Duff said, rolling over with a creak of his cot.

"You are, Duff," Danny said gently to his already snoring friend. "You are."

EIGHT

THERE WERE NOW enough bits of information about the case that Sherlock Holmes called for a meeting of the Baker Street Brigade. Peachy slipped out through the gates of the Tower and made his way to the top of Tower Hill. Holmes met him there in a growler that already carried Danny and Duff.

On the ride back to Baker Street, Peachy told of his night's investigations, the strange actions of the raven master and the finding of the bit of code. Danny brought Peachy up to date on the failure of the bookie's marker to progress them further, other than the strange piece of news about the Dutch coin. And finally, since the boys were so completely involved in the case, Holmes told them what had been stolen and why secrecy was so important. "We must not scare them off," he concluded, "or all is lost."

Once inside the parlor, Holmes set to work on the code, which he said was the best and freshest item of information they had. As always, Peachy was fascinated by the contrast between the detective's intellect and calculating mind and the cluttered, messy look of his rooms. A sheaf of unpaid bills was speared to the fireplace mantel by an open jackknife, and foul-smelling pipe tobacco spilled from a Persian slipper hanging nearby.

Holmes scratched another mark on the already cluttered blackboard below the drawing of Peachy's discovery. Duff, Peachy, and Danny stood in a semicircle watching. The private investigator tried multiple versions of code solutions he had discovered over the many years of his practice. He tried the formula where *e* is the most frequently used letter in the alphabet and the other letters appear in decreasing frequency, but got nowhere. "Blast!" Holmes spouted. "It won't do! Won't do at all!" He then attempted to apply another character-grouping theory, as well as half a dozen others. "Hang it all, boys. If I can't solve a simple decoding problem, how will we get to the bottom of this?" Holmes shrieked. "Carnehan, are you certain this is exactly the way you found it?"

"That's it," Peachy replied solidly. "Observation, you know." Holmes shot the boy a look that was half irritation and half amusement.

"If only we had the first sequence." Sherlock said, pouting. "The one Danny and Duff found."

Duff cocked his head sideways on his shoulder like a chicken inspecting a bug as a potential meal, then took a step toward the blackboard. "Mr. Holmes," he said softly, "I 'member those marks you's talking about."

Holmes stopped writing, slowly turning to Duff and regarding the boy with an appraising eye. "You do?" he asked, encouraging Duff to go on. "Can you draw them for me?"

"Sure," Duff answered confidently, reaching for the chalk. Duff took the small powdery stick and began drawing the characters on the dry piece of slate. He never hesitated, but wrote them down straight through to the end. The chalk squeaked so that Peachy wanted to cover his ears, but Duff seemed not to notice.

"Duff," Danny said. "Why didn't you tell us this before, mate?"

Duff, sounding completely unconcerned, replied, "Nobody asked me."

Like the message Peachy found, all the figures were square in shape. Some were completely closed, and some were two- or three-sided. The message looked like this:

Holmes rested his chin on his hand, while watching intently. When Duff finished, he gently set the chalk down and took a step backward. All four stared blankly at the sequence of marks that Duff had masterfully reproduced.

"It looks like mine," Peachy commented. "Only different."

"Yes," Holmes agreed. "What an amazing memory you have, Duff," Holmes congratulated. "One might almost call it photographic."

"You like it?" Duff asked hopefully.

"I do, I do, Duff. It's truly remarkable." Then the detective added, "But I don't know that it makes it any easier to decipher."

Duff seemed disappointed and he lowered his head.

Danny squinted at the board, while Peachy turned his head sideways, back and forth. Nothing seemed to help.

"I don't know if we can be of any more use to you, Mr. Holmes," Danny informed sadly.

Holmes spoke up. "That's all right, my little wharf rats. I've more to work from than I would have, if not for your efforts. Find something to occupy yourselves, while I continue thinking. Mrs. Hudson will be along shortly with tea and biscuits."

"Cheerio, then," Danny responded. "Does anyone want to play a game? How about tick-tack-toe?"

"Sure," Peachy said, grabbing a pencil and a sheet of paper from the detective's cluttered desk.

Down twice, two long lines, and to the right twice Peachy marked, making the board on which they were to play. Danny started and both boys fired their choices rapidly. An *X* in the center box, countered by an *O* in the top right. Three more marks from each, and the game was a draw.

"Let's have another go," Danny said.

Peachy, sensing something clicking in his brain, but not sure what, looked from the game to the blackboard where Holmes stood pondering the code. Peachy studied the characters in the messages, and then took another hard look at the game. Flashing back and forth from the game to the cryptic writing, Peachy noticed the similarity in the shape of the square figures to the corners and center of the play surface.

"Mr. Holmes," Peachy said slowly, not wanting to jump to a wrong conclusion and disturb the great detective, "I think I see something."

Sherlock Holmes heard the serious tone of the boy's words and pivoted with his eyebrows raised.

Wordlessly, Peachy turned the sheet on which the game was drawn so that Holmes could see, then the boy pointed to the shapes on the blackboard.

Instantly the investigator grasped the connection. "Nine boxes," Holmes counted. "And by using them with and without dots, that would make eighteen combinations. However," he sighed, looking distressed, "twenty-six letters in the alphabet . . . that leaves eight unaccounted for."

The detective looked at the codes written in front of him, noticing the one- and two-figure words in each. "That's it!" he exclaimed. "There are no vowels in this code."

As the Irregulars watched with astonishment, Holmes drew the code key on the board with a flurry of strokes and flying chalk dust.

B C	D F	G H
J K	L M	N P
Q R	S T	V W

"Now then," Holmes said, finishing. "Let us see if it works. By omitting the vowels and disregarding *X, Y,* and *Z* as unnecessary, I think we can make this fit. You see, the top left-hand corner is *B* if without a dot or *C* if the dot is used."

Once more the chalk dashed across the slate and the message PCK P T SLT TWR emerged.

"But that still doesn't mean anything," Peachy complained.

Holmes wagged his finger to warn Peachy to hold on. "Remember, we must add back the missing vowels. The first word could be *PACK, PECK, POCK,* or even someone's name. And notice here," he said, pointing to the new code, and the last three symbols of each. "See how they're exactly alike. These three might be the grouping for the word *Tower.*"

"That's it," Peachy shouted. "You've cooled it for fair! SLT must be the word *Salt* for *Salt Tower.*"

"And," Danny exclaimed, jumping into the decoding, "PCK P T could mean *Pick Up At!*"

"Exquisite," Holmes said, stepping back to admire their accomplishment. "Now let's figure out last night's message, and hope it provides us with a new lead."

The boys watched as the detective repeated the process, deciphering the code once more.

"BCK F RVS TWR," Peachy sounded out. "Back of raven's tower."

"But there is no raven's tower," Danny protested.

"But maybe it means the wall closest to the raven's pen. That would be the . . ." Peachy paused and consulted his memory of excursions inside the fort. "That would be the Wakefield Tower."

"Crikey, I bet you're right," Danny agreed. "It means the area of the raven's pen nearest the Wakefield Tower, but it was a shorter way to say it like."

"My congratulations, boys, but the case is not yet solved," Holmes announced. "We still have to find the man responsible for switching the jewels, and today is the perfect day to keep watch. Peachy, you and Danny go to the Tower ceremony being held for the diplomats to see their gifts on display. I will come later. Keep watch and note anything, or anyone, suspicious."

"Right-o," Peachy agreed, feeling proud.

"Duff, you will come with me disguised as a worker to check out the back of the ravens' cage for clues. I'll need your memory in case we find any more messages," Holmes said.

Duff, who had remained silent through the celebrating over the code, also swelled with happiness. "I'll do good," he promised.

"Keep a sharp eye out, boys," Holmes instructed Peachy and Danny. "Mrs. Hudson!" he called sharply. "I'll need some large overalls from my wardrobe, if you please. Two pair from the steamer trunk in the attic."

————

The bony hand of Sherlock Holmes rapped solidly on the small oak viewing panel of the Tower's outer portal. Duff stood behind him, patiently holding a wooden troughed toolbox. The view port slid to one side, revealing the pointed red nose and rosy cheeks of the warder who kept watch behind. " 'Oo goes there?" he grunted at Holmes.

The foul smell of bitter brew and plowman's lunch of cheese and pickle wafted through the small square slot. Holmes gasped, rolling his eyes. "I coom to fix the birds' cage. I hear they scootin' out all over the place."

"Bird cage," the guard repeated, pressing his face to the hole and thoroughly examining them both.

"Yuss," Holmes replied, checking his mustache disguise with his index finger. It had slipped down a tiny bit and he pressed it back in place. The shaggy, dirty blond whiskers matched the shaggy, dirty blond wig that stuck out all around the detective's head.

" 'Oo's 'ee?" the sentry asked, pointing at Duff.

"He's wit me. Me little helper, he is," Holmes replied.

The man wiped his mouth on the cuff of his uniform, sniffed like a horse, then continued to wipe on up his sleeve. " 'Ee don't look so little to me." Puckering his lips in consideration, the guard looked again at Duff. Then he chuckled, belched, and nodded his agreement. "Come in, then, mate."

The overweight guard rubbed his sweaty red hair. "You be-n't English, eh? What in dog's blight's your lingo? What country are you from anyway?"

"My moother is Dutch, and me father is Welch. I guess that makes me Delch. Hee, hee, hee." Holmes laughed a dry, raspy cackle which the guard did not immediately join, although Duff did.

The warder stared strangely at the detective who limped past the gate. "Uh, huh," the guard sputtered. "Now I get it. Delch, ha!" The man finished chuckling with a bullfrog belch.

Duff's shoulders swayed from side to side from the weight of the heavy toolbox. The man walked Holmes right up to the next guard box. "Thatcher, take good care of these Delch boys," he said, laughing. "And give 'em no trouble." The red-faced guard waved and shuffled off laughing.

"We be fine from here, dank you," Holmes informed the sentry. "I know where I be goin'." Duff proceeded through with Holmes, clanking the toolbox against his leg.

At the north side of the Wakefield Tower, Holmes checked around, then slipped covertly into the raven yard. Since it was day and not feeding time, the ravens were spread across the grounds and not in their enclosure. Duff tried to follow as furtively as Holmes, but banged the heavy trough against a post. Clanging metal rang like a fire alarm, and the wrenches jumped and rattled, before Holmes grabbed him by the arm and pulled him in.

"My dear boy," he cautioned, "I don't think you can expect to spy with a red flag waving above your head."

Duff turned three complete circles while looking up for the flag that Holmes spoke of. "I don't see no flag," Duff said, "and what'll I do with these tools?"

"Just put them down," Holmes replied patiently. "What I need you to do right now is keep watch for others."

The investigator searched the raven area and the nearby walls for clues. He dug through the straw, finding nothing. Duff watched the walkways for a while, but found studying the detective's funny behavior, crawling on hands and knees, more entertaining. Holmes entered the nesting shed.

A few minutes passed and then Duff heard a voice behind them say, "If only I had my hands on them jewels right now, I'd kiss all you little beggars good-bye." Glancing toward the entrance, Duff was startled by the sudden appearance of George Fenton, the raven master.

"Mr. Holmes," Duff nervously called.

Fenton squinted at Duff from his coal-black eyes, down his beak-like nose. He walked closer, staring angrily. "What be you doing to my birds?"

"Mr. Holmes," Duff tried again, still without response.

Fenton moved closer yet, calculating each footstep and staring as if trying to place where he had seen Duff.

Duff took several steps backward before falling over a rake. "Help!" Duff screamed.

"What in heaven's name is wrong?" Holmes yelled, reappearing again from inside the coop.

"What in blazes are you doin' in my bird cage?" Fenton yelled. He apparently did not recognize Holmes.

"Egg inspector. We're checking to see how many eggs you have," Holmes answered calmly.

"How many eggs I have?" Fenton repeated, puzzled. "What for?"

"It's a new law," Holmes said sternly. "First the window tax, and now a tax on eggs."

"What?" Fenton said with confusion.

Holmes took a step past him, moving toward the gate. "Oh yes, it's a heinous, punishable crime to underreport egg production. It seems as though you haven't paid."

"But I didn't know," Fenton squeaked, "and these aren't my birds anyway. And besides, there be-n't any eggs."

"So I have seen," Holmes said, as he motioned for Duff to pick up the tools. "You are very lucky . . . this time." He and Duff headed up toward Tower Green.

"What if there were eggs?" Fenton called. "What should I do?"

"If I were you, I'd break them," was the reply.

NINE

THE GREAT HALL at the top floor of the White Tower was filled with chattering, as diplomats from all over the world examined the accumulated presentations of respect and admiration for Queen Victoria. The vaulted stone ceiling carried even whispers clearly, as Lord Frith began his official speech of welcome. "Good day. On behalf of our gracious Queen Victoria, and her kingdom, I would like to thank all of you who have brought gifts to the throne for her Fiftieth Year Golden Jubilee Celebration. Because tomorrow will be a very busy and formal schedule, Her Majesty wishes to give you the special privilege of seeing the collection of priceless gifts. Be at your leisure to look around and enjoy the refreshments. Thank you, and God save the queen." Lord Frith stepped down from the lectern and the crowd returned to the previous noisy level of conversation. At the back of the room, near a serving door, Danny and Peachy kept watch as Holmes had instructed.

"Crikey! There's people from all over the world here," Peachy remarked with amazement.

"I saw the American ambassador over by the Duke of Aosta, the brother of the King of Spain," Danny said, pointing to the oversized gold and silver punch bowl, brought from Spain.

"How did you know who they was?" Peachy questioned.

Danny tossed a handful of roasted nuts into his mouth. "I saw pictures in the paper a couple of days ago. I observed."

"Hey," Peachy exclaimed, nudging Danny's leg with the back of his hand, "I heard that in the middle of all these fancy gifts, the Emperor of China sent two boxes of tea."

"Ha, ha," Danny laughed. "Really?"

"Serious as a headsman's ax," Peachy insisted.

"Prob'ly get used when all these other things is catching dust," Danny mused.

"Hey, Danny," Peachy asked, looking down at a printed guest list. "What kind of a place is Borneo?"

Danny chuckled. "I don't know. What's a Sarawak?"

Peachy shrugged. "I've got one for ya," he continued.

Danny gave a nod. "Right-o, fire away then, mate."

"What do they call a Bolivian when he dies?" Carnehan asked.

Danny raised his brows. "I don't know, what?"

Peachy snickered. "A Bo-dead-ian!"

Danny was unsure if the joke was really funny or just really stupid, but he was laughing anyway when he asked, "What do you suppose they do in the Sunda Islands?"

"Carnehan, Wiggins," Holmes called as he and

Duff approached, having changed out of their disguises once again. "Have you recognized our man yet?"

"Not yet," Peachy noted, scratching his cheek. "But we was just wondering: what are the Sunda Islands?"

"It's part of Sumatra, in the East Indies," Holmes replied. "It's a Dutch colony, famous for coffee and pearls and monkeys . . ." Holmes grew surprisingly silent and he stared blankly.

"I like monkeys," Duff said. "I seed some at the zoo in Regent's Park."

"That may be it," Holmes said, snapping out of it.

"A monkey stealing jewels?" Peachy asked.

Holmes ignored the response and asked a question of his own. "Is there a Sumatran diplomat here?"

"Could be," Danny answered, scanning the guest list again.

Holmes grew so agitated that his explanation sounded garbled. "The gold coin," he said, "at the bookie shop. What's his name?" He snapped impatiently, "The coin was Dutch. Hurry, tell me, what is his name?"

Holmes snatched the printed program out of Danny's hands. Flipping through the pages, he read aloud as he scanned the list, his finger moving in rapid jerks down the register. "Queen Kapiolani, Hawaii. Hessen el Sultaneh, Persia. Nels Van Rorin . . . Sumatra. Nels Van Rorin," Holmes murmured under his breath. Looking to see if anyone had overheard, he closed the program and gestured to the boys. "Come, lads. We'll talk outside."

On a bench on Tower Green, where only a raven could listen in, Holmes filled in the gaps. "My Irregulars, listen closely to what I have planned. This character Nels—I need you and Duff, Danny, to follow him to his hotel. Once there, send for me, and I'll be along quickly. Meanwhile, I'll keep an eye on things here."

Danny thought about the plan, then asked, "But if he's the knapper, why don't you collar him now?"

"It's too soon," he explained. "An early arrest may forfeit the goods they already have. Without a doubt, another attempt will be made tonight. Tomorrow the gifts will be moved to St. James Palace, Exhibition Hall, where their inside man will be of no further use. If we time this properly, we will bag the lot and recover the stolen gems!"

"What'll I do, then, sir?" Peachy asked, feeling left out.

"We must still identify the inside man," the detective reminded Peachy. "So you need to continue your watch. Also, Duff and I searched the ravens' yard without results, but I still have my suspicions," Holmes said, flicking his hands. "Keep an eye on the area. Apply pressure to Fenton, the raven master, by hanging around, but don't give away any information that might put him on the run, understand?"

"Got it, Holmes," Peachy said crisply. Surprised at his slip-up, he covered his lips with his hands, then apologized. "Sorry, uh, Mr. Holmes."

"Good man, Peachy." Holmes said, nodding. "Wiggins, Bernard, here's cab fare. I'll wait your return in the Hall. Now go. Van Rorin will be leaving soon."

————

"Follow that cart, sir," Danny told the driver of the hansom cab as he jumped in and slammed the door. Nels Van Rorin's carriage had just pulled away from the Tower's drive. Cabs and carriages and carts so crowded the London streets that unless they left at once on his trail, the Sumatran dignitary would be impossible to trace.

"Not half," the cabby said, mocking Danny's serious tone. "What are you two playin' at, then? Coppers and buzzers, eh?"

"It's really urgent," Danny said, showing his fistful of money. "Half a crown over if you keep it in sight."

"Right-o, guvnor," the cabbie agreed, pulling on his cap and whipping up the horse.

The two cabs headed down Lower Thames Street, past the sprawling Billingsgate Market, the aroma indicating what was sold there even before Danny caught sight of the fish-shaped weather vanes. They continued on to Upper Thames Street, always traveling west along the river. Several miles down the road the highway came to the Embankment. A short while later the black carriage pulled up at the Savoy Hotel. Danny instructed the driver of the cab to pull over half a block behind. As soon as he saw Van Rorin enter the lobby of the swank lodging, he and Duff got out.

"Here ya go, guvnor," the driver said, locking the reins into the spiraled metal clasp. "That'll be eighty p, if you please."

Jumping out, Danny handed him seven shillings, worth eighty-four pence and the promised half crown coin worth thirty pence more. "Could you wait?"

The cabby took the handful of money and tipped his hat. "Why not?" He chuckled. "It may turn out to be int'resting. You gen'lmen mind your manners in there." He pointed with his whip at the motel. "Blimey, they don't even let the likes of me go in there. But don't let 'em give you no grief."

Danny thanked him and rushed to the entrance with Duff. Inside, brightly lit ceilings dripped with enormous crystal chandeliers. Across the lobby, fifteen servants, bellmen, doormen, and porters, all suited in green waistcoats and black trousers, moved about with quiet efficiency.

Danny watched as Nels Van Rorin approached the counter to get his key.

"Mr. Van Rorin," the clerk greeted the man. "Room 267, I believe."

"Yes it is, thank you," Van Rorin replied, collecting the key.

"267, 267," Danny whispered to himself. "Duff, you wait over here," he instructed, placing his friend just outside the entrance, "while I go get Mr. Holmes. If Van Rorin leaves again before we return, follow him and send word back here."

"Cheerio." Duff nodded. "I can do that."

"I'll be back soon," Danny said confidently. He jumped into the cab once more and this time the driver said with a respectful smile, "Where to, guvnor?"

"Back to the Tower," Danny said, tapping on the ceiling of the compartment as he had seen Holmes do.

The driver chuckled, cracking the reins. "Now how did I tumble he was gonna say that?"

————

The warm afternoon sun beat down on Tower Green. Things had slowed down considerably after the reception finished. Peachy strolled lazily over from the White Tower to where the headsman's block stood on the grass, surrounded by a low fence. While sitting on a bench, he thought about how fun it was to be the chief warder's nephew, at least for a time anyway. From his spot on the bench he could study the ravens' pen, though George Fenton was nowhere to be seen.

"Hello, boy," one of the yeoman warders greeted him. Because of the presence of all the distinguished guests, the warders were in their dress uniforms. A bright red tunic trimmed in gold bore the embroidered rose, shamrock, and thistle design that represented Britain, Ireland, and Scotland, beneath a golden crown.

"Hello," Peachy said, nodding, remembering how he'd gathered half of the guards under his thumb by getting dirt about all of them. "Cheerio," he said, waving to another, as a raven swooped down from the barred windows of the White Tower.

Peachy watched it as it flew low over the green, down to its cage near the Wakefield Tower. When it had landed, Peachy looked again to the metal grating that covered the windows of the Great Hall where the gifts were stored. Another bird edged out on the windowsill and jumped, just the same as the other one had. Peachy studied it as it flew past him.

A closer inspection showed that the jet-black bird carried something small and white in its tightly curled claw. *Could it be,* he wondered, *after all this time, could it be the birds that carried out this dirty crime? Had they been trained to steal the gems?*

The raven coasted smoothly, descending to the pen, where it landed inside the enclosure. Peachy, frowning as he hurriedly stood, rushed down the walk to investigate. As he neared the pen, not more than ten feet away, George Fenton appeared.

The raven master pushed the wire gate open and walked to the nesting area where he said, "Come here, ya little beggar. What did ya bring me today?" Fenton was unaware that Peachy had overheard him and even now stood watching to see what would happen next.

Peachy tiptoed closer to the fence where he could see in through the door of the wooden hut. There, in the dark, Fenton struggled with the bird, which was reluctant to let go of its treasure.

"Gimme that pretty, you little buzzer, or I'll stuff you for my mantle," Fenton threatened, continuing to wrestle with the sharp talons and beak of the bird.

A flash caught Peachy's eye from the thing that the bird concealed in its claw. *A gem,* he thought. It had to be. Fenton must be sending the birds in to get the stuff, then bringing the fakes in later to replace them.

The raven master pulled something loose from the raven, stuffing a small object in his pocket. Turning around, he was startled by Peachy's presence. " 'Ow long you been there, ya little squint?" Fenton blustered.

"Long enough," Peachy said, "to see that you're stealing jewels."

"Whaaaat?" the raven master screamed. "Stealing jewels? I ought to tan your hide for such a yarn, ya little brat."

Peachy, frightened, took a step back. "I saw how you do it," he announced. "I saw the birds come right through that barred window over there." Peachy pointed to the window in the White Tower. "And it brought you that jewel that you just took from it."

"Ha!" Fenton laughed loudly, ducking his head at Peachy. "You mean *this* jewel?" he said, reaching into his pocket. "There, looky there." He guffawed. "How much ya think a piece of chalk like this is worth anyhow?"

Peachy stared with embarrassment as Fenton held

the bit of white chalk up high, rolling it around between his fingers.

"There's your jewel!" Fenton cackled as he threw the chalk at Peachy. "He's stolen someone's school tablet, he has!" The raven master brushed off the fine powder on the seat of his uniform, leaving a white stain atop the red and gold fabric.

Peachy rolled his eyes and wondered how he could have been so stupid.

"Get outta here, ya lousy chavvy," Fenton cursed. He roughly shoved Peachy away from the pen, then turned and stalked off.

——————

When Danny and Holmes returned to the Strand, they had collected Scotland Yard's Chief Inspector Avery, and over an hour had passed. They found a gloomy Duff sitting on the curb outside the Savoy Hotel, in the U-shaped courtyard where the carriages turn around.

Holmes frowned as he leaped down from the cab. "Duff, what happened?"

"They threw me out, Mr. Holmes," Duff said as a tear welled up in his eye.

"Where's Van Rorin?"

"He's gone," Duff said, through his sniffles.

"Gone? Wiggins, quickly. What was the room again?"

"Two sixty-seven," Danny said.

"This way, gentlemen," Holmes called, bursting into the lobby with Inspector Avery and a half dozen other officers of the Metropolitan Police Force.

Inspector Avery stopped at reception to present his credentials and explain, demanding the key for Van

Rorin's room. Danny and Duff led Holmes up two flights of stairs.

"Over here," Danny called, stopping in front of room 267.

At a nod from the inspector, the key was turned and two large constables crashed through the opening. Holmes and the boys marched in after as the policemen spread out through the several rooms of the suite.

One of the Bobbies came back out of the master bedroom. "It's empty, sir," the man reported to Avery. "He's flown."

"Blast!" Sherlock Holmes yelled. "Avery, with your permission: have your men check the closets, under the carpets, and in the waste bins. Every speck must be examined."

Shortly, all the officers returned to the living area with its large beveled-glass mirror above a marble-faced fireplace. "It's clean," one said. "Nothing," another informed. "Bloke took all his trash with him even."

"Gone," Holmes commented with resignation, looking to Duff. "How did this happen?"

"The man we was following didn't come out the front where I was and you and Danny didn't come back, so I went into the spin-around glass door and I said to the chap behind the desk did he know where the bloke went we was looking for and that's when they throwed me out. I watched the front, just like Danny told me," Duff said. "But he didn't never come out."

Inspector Avery, who had gone to question the desk clerk, returned from the lobby and entered the room. Placing his hands on his hips, he said sternly, "Van Rorin checked out and left through the side door. He had another carriage waiting already when he first arrived. There was nothing one man could have done to watch every exit," he said, nodding at Duff. "Van Rorin seems to have planned his departure to throw off any pursuit."

Holmes asked if Van Rorin had said anything else to the desk clerk or if the clerk remembered any messages for the man.

"Only one," Avery said. "The clerk recalled putting a telegram for Van Rorin in his box."

"What did it say?"

Inspector Avery shook his head. "The reception manager only recollected that it said something about a boat and Cubitt Town."

"That's all?" Holmes questioned.

"Nothing else," Avery answered. "Now what, Holmes? You still haven't told me what this is all about. What is the dreadful urgency about catching this one man?"

"Tonight, Inspector Avery," the private investigator spoke softly. "We may just have one more chance to apprehend him. Have a dozen men and two of your fastest steam launches docked near Tower Wharf, but out of sight. Have them fueled up and ready to go. If we are successful, perhaps I will be able to explain. If not, every newspaper in the civilized world will present you with the story, and it will not be pleasant reading."

TEN

A BREEZE FROM the river picked up as Peachy walked aimlessly up the stairs to the top of the Brass Mount, outside of the Martin Tower. Built in the year 1275 by order of King Edward I, the Brass Mount was the northeasternmost corner of the Tower. Designed to let archers cover Tower Hill, the Brass Mount was one of the largest towers in diameter. From the top, Peachy looked over the green marsh of what had once been the water of the moat. Filled in during 1852, the low ground around the outer walls remained a wet and smelly swamp.

Peachy's mind began to churn. Though Peachy was embarrassed about jumping to conclusions, when he reviewed the episode with the raven and the chalk from earlier that day, he still wondered if George Fenton had been up to something. Even though it was a piece of chalk the raven master had produced, could he not have left the real gem in his pocket?

Wandering south along the outer wall, Peachy paused a moment when he reached the Develin Tower.

The southeastern corner, it provided a panorama of the river. The boy watched a small gray fishing boat pass through the footings of the unfinished Tower Bridge, much the same view as he had from the Lanthorn Tower a few nights before.

Peachy made his way down the steps and onto Water Lane. A shiver ran down his spine as he approached Lanthorn Tower, recalling his bad experience on the rooftop at night. Maybe he did believe in ghosts, he thought. There was so much that was eerie around this place.

The boy was roused from his thoughts when he saw a man in the uniform of a guards officer approaching through the gap between St. Thomas's Tower and the Wakefield Tower. The officer smiled at Peachy and he returned his smile as they drew nearer.

The man waved as they passed. "You are Chief Gladstone's nephew," the man stated. "I'm Captain Frith. I hope you enjoy your visit to the castle," he concluded before walking on down the lane. He seemed friendly enough, but preoccupied.

An alarm bell began to ring in Peachy's head. The sense of danger was so great that the boy turned around, expecting to see the raven master or another grim form. But the only thing in sight was the retreating back of Captain Frith.

Peachy stopped to watch the officer. There was something about the man that caught the boy's attention. Peachy could not say what it was, but he slipped out of sight behind an angle of the stone wall in order to continue his study undetected.

Sure enough, when Frith reached the archway by the Salt Tower he looked all around, as if making certain that he was not being observed. But the captain did not see Peachy, and the boy was now more curious than ever. Then Frith turned a sharp left to pass through the inner wall. As he did so the captain idly dusted his hand against the seat of his trousers.

It was in that instant that two things leapt into sharp focus for Peachy: it was a smudge of white chalk dust that the man wiped on his black uniform pants and . . . as the figure turned to his left, his pale profile was framed against the dark stone of the arch. It was the gambling soldier from Cubitt Town!

Peachy's heart pounded. "If he *is* the one, then he probably just left another message. Maybe he's even going to get the jewels right now," Peachy noted aloud to himself.

Examining both ends of Water Lane before stopping near Traitors' Gate, Peachy noticed that no other guards were in sight—not in the lane, nor on the outer wall near the river, nor patrolling inside. A few minutes of searching revealed a new set of coded instructions, freshly chalked on the lowest stone on the corner of the Bloody Tower. No time to decipher it now! Peachy decided to go get Warder Gladstone and tell him all that he knew or suspected.

In a full sprint he took off, rounded the corner and ran headfirst into Frith's chest. "Ahhh!" Peachy screamed as Frith grabbed his arms.

"What's wrong?" Frith asked. "Seen a ghost?"

"Ghosts," Peachy agreed, stuttering. "I get afraid of all these ghosts down here."

"There's a lot of them," Frith agreed. "Maybe you'd better go home where it's safe."

"Yes, sir," Peachy concurred. "I think you're right."

"Run along," Captain Frith said, letting go of Peachy's arms.

Peachy ran like a hound on a hunt, or rather, like the fox being chased by a whole pack of hounds. All the way up to Tower Green he sprinted, searching all around for Chief Warder Gladstone and looking over his shoulder to see if Frith had changed his mind and was pursuing him. But when he neared the top of the slope, he found Sherlock Holmes, Danny, and Duff.

"Carnehan," Holmes called, "where are you running to in such haste?"

"To find someone," Peachy panted, out of breath. Then with relief he added, "To find you."

"What's wrong, Peachy?" Holmes asked, stooping his lean frame to the boy's height.

"Down, down by the water . . . I saw Frith . . . and another message . . . and he's the man, the man from Cubitt Town!" Peachy puffed.

"Where is he now?" Holmes asked quickly, looking to see if Frith was around.

"He's down there still," Peachy said, exhausted. "Or just was!" The boy shuddered again at the memory of his recent encounter.

"Right," Holmes said with authority. "Danny, you go and get Chief Warder Gladstone from his house. Tell him to meet me in St. Peter's Chapel where we'll have a view across the whole square. We'll nab Frith when he comes out." Holmes gave his instructions in a calm tone, as if he were reading them from a book.

————

Stacks of rusty medieval instruments of torture cluttered the dark dungeon floor of the Martin Tower. Thumbscrews and knotted cords, clubs and iron fetters, unused for centuries, were stored in the dank hole. The

Brigade and Holmes stood quietly around an oval table, flanking Chief Warder Gladstone. At the head of the table sat Captain Frith, looking stricken, while behind him stood two hefty, grim-faced yeoman warders. Frith was speechless and stared straight ahead.

"The ploy is up, Frith. We know about the robbery," Gladstone intoned.

"I don't know anything about any robbery," Frith pleaded.

Holmes and the others had stayed concealed within St. Peter's Chapel. Exactly as the detective had predicted, Frith had emerged from the White Tower by way of a little used side entrance. When caught, he had been in possession of a pocketful of jewels. It made his denials ludicrous and flat.

"You bring in the fakes, then smuggle out the valuables. Right?" Gladstone yelled.

"No," Frith argued, "you don't understand."

"Give it up!" Gladstone warned. "We know you owed the bookies a lot of money. We also know that you have been leaving different coded messages for your accomplices. You have betrayed your queen, your country, and your oath. Do you think that any defense will excuse all that?"

Frith still sat mute and unmoving.

Everyone waited for Holmes to speak and when he did not they looked to see why. The investigator seemed to be ignoring the criminal and studying something in the darkest corner of the room. Peachy peered into the blackness and saw immense wooden wheels, pulleys, and ropes that dangled loosely from a wooden frame.

Holmes turned to Gladstone casually. "It does not look like the rack has been in use recently."

"That's so," Gladstone agreed. "There has not been a need . . . until now."

Peachy turned his eyes away from the torture device and looked again at Frith. Streams of sweat rolled down Frith's face and he whimpered.

"The only hope for you now is to cooperate fully," Gladstone said. "We must have names and details and we must have them at once."

"Please, sir," Frith pleaded, "I didn't mean to, I mean, I didn't have a choice, or the bookies would have killed me. There was nothing I could do, so I . . ."

"Be silent. No more excuses," Holmes demanded.

"Yes, sir," Frith sobbed.

Turning to Danny, Holmes said, "Wiggins, you and the warder take Frith's keys and run to the Great Hall. Switch the real jewels for the fakes again, and bring the counterfeits back here."

Danny grabbed the keys from the table and sprinted out the door with the bag.

Holmes, his slender finger resting beside his chin, paced around the table. "So that you will not try to deceive us, let me tell you how much we already know," he explained. "Then you will tell us the rest, or it will go very ill with you indeed. You, Ronald Frith, son of Lord Frith of Rochester, falsely obtained a bank draft on your father's account. Foolishly betting the money on a rigged horse race, you lost it all. Instead of embarrassing your father with your theft and the loss, you then borrowed money on a marker from the bookies, hoping to make good your losses and replace the stolen funds. But when you lost again, and could not repay the loan, the bookmakers threatened you with your life. When someone you had never met before approached you and indicated willingness to settle your debts, you fell into the clutches of Nels Van Rorin and became his cat's-paw in the theft of the gifts. Only uncut stones and plain gold pieces, easily duplicated, were chosen for stealing. You carried out the plot by taking the fakes into the White Tower by an unused spiral stair to which you alone, as a captain of the guard, had the key. You then left the real gems for collection in a place designated by you in code. Have I said anything incorrect?"

Frith shook his head pathetically.

Holmes stopped pacing next to Frith. Leaning down close to his ear he said softly, "Now, Ronald Frith, as of this moment you are working for me."

"But they'll kill me," Frith screamed, squirming free from the guard and jumping to his feet.

Chief Gladstone swung around, and resurrecting a twenty-pound mace from the dust of the dungeon, bashed Frith in the head with the heavy birch handle. Frith fell face first to the table.

Sherlock grabbed a handful of Frith's hair and raised the man's face to look him in the eye. "Now, what was the plan for tonight?"

Frith steadied himself, completely submissive and cooperative. "Since the gifts were all to be moved tomorrow," he said, "tonight was the last haul. Instead of someone coming to retrieve the jewels, I was to take them down myself for collection."

Holmes looked suspicious. "Be careful, Frith," he warned. "Do not trifle with me. Why did you write a new message then?"

"I'm not lying!" Frith protested. "This message said I wanted to go with them. I knew I was going to get caught," he concluded miserably.

"Go where? When?" Gladstone interrupted impatiently.

"I don't know! Van Rorin never told me!"

Holmes pointed his finger into Frith's face. "Here is what you will do," he said. "You will take the fakes to the rendezvous, as if you'd switched them. You will not speak a word," Holmes instructed, "but will remain composed and do as you are told."

"Yes sir," he moaned. "I'll say nothing."

"Be certain of it!" Gladstone yelled, swinging the heavy spiked ball of the mace into the soft pine table, splintering a fist-sized hole in front of Frith. "Or you'll be stretched from the rack, before you're hanged from the gallows!"

Holmes turned to Peachy. "Carnehan, go with Warder Burles. Wait in the window of the Bloody Tower for Frith's meeting. Listen closely from the window to what he says and report to me after it is done.

"Yes, Mr. Holmes," Peachy answered.

"Burles, take your Martini rifle with you; ready your sights on him, and listen for my command. If he loses composure or hints in any way as to what has happened, you will please shoot him."

Frith swallowed hard, knowing he had no other choice if he wanted to live.

"Yes, sir," Warder Burles agreed. He and Peachy made a hasty exit.

Gladstone nodded to Holmes. "You and I can wait on the walk above St. Thomas's Tower, nearest the river."

"Precisely," Holmes exclaimed, as Danny and the other guard returned with the bag of fake jewels.

"Excellent speed, Wiggins," Sherlock commended.

"You and Duff shall keep watch from the top of Wakefield Tower. Look for the ship and try to make out its features. If they accept the fakes, then we can follow to their hideout and collect the lot—stolen gems and criminals all."

ELEVEN

A BLACK NIGHT hung damply over the smooth, rounded cobblestones of the Bloody Tower courtyard. The water of the river lapped gently against Traitors' Gate. The hours passed slowly while Peachy and Warder Burles waited in silence for the exchange to take place. Who, or what, would take the jewels, they had not a clue.

Through the wavy, leaded glass panes, Peachy barely blinked while watching the lane below. Behind the boy, in the unlighted room where legend said the little princes were murdered, Warder Burles sat with his loaded rifle. The marksman studied the distance to the water's edge, adjusted the sights, checked the elevation and prepared another cartridge on the floor beside him. About every fifteen minutes he went through the whole process again.

"Crikey! That's a ream sharp blade," Peachy said, reaching out toward the bayonet that lay beside Burles on the floor.

"Never touch another man's weapon," Burles

scolded. "I'll bet you don't even granny what a rifle'll do, or even a small gun for that matter."

"Sorry," Peachy apologized.

"I forgive you, but it ain't all right. Hark to me, lad: you can't tell if a barker is loaded or not, and even if it ain't, you don't know what the jack who owns it'll do, if he catches you messin' about." Burles finished his lecture and returned to his quarterhour's inspection.

———

"Still no sign," Gladstone whispered to Holmes. "I hope they didn't get wind of what's happened."

Holmes squinted at his pocket watch. "He'll show, I assure you."

"I hope you're right," Gladstone commented, resuming his observation of the river.

"My good man, I am always right," Holmes joked. "And if he doesn't come, we'll shoot Frith just the same."

Gladstone frowned, looking at Holmes as if uncertain that it was a joke. "I wonder if the boys have seen anything yet?" he said, turning around to get a glimpse of the Wakefield Tower's roof.

———

Danny could barely make out anything against the silted black water of the Thames. Duff sighed, turned his back to the wall overlooking the river, and slid down to stretch out his legs.

"What's wrong, Duff?" Danny asked.

"Aren't those guys never gonna come?"

"Blimey," Danny said, "we're about to solve a blooming mystery! Aren't you excited?" Then some movement on the water caught his eye. "Wait, I see something!"

Duff scrambled up to see what it was.

"Stay low," Danny ordered, pushing Duff's big head down behind the battlements. "Peek through here. See it? There, between that farthest footing of Tower Bridge and the other bank."

"That little boat?" Duff replied. "That shiny thing out there? What are they doin'?"

"I'm not certain," Danny replied. "It looks like they're putting something in the water." The frame of a hoist and a boom swung out from the ship and lowered its cargo into the river.

Danny licked his lips and leaned farther into the casemate in order to obtain a better view.

Duff blinked continuously, as if the excitement was too much for him. "What are them cables, Danny? Are they fishin'?"

Outside Traitors' Gate, beneath the surface of the river, bubbles began to pop up.

"Duff, look!" Danny whispered.

An egg-shaped object with half spheres bulging from the top lifted up in the pool beneath steps down from Traitors' Gate. A soft puttering noise reached Danny's ears as bubbles rose and popped, reminding the boy of Holmes's chemistry lab at Baker Street.

————

Peachy saw Holmes signal with his hand for Warder Burles to ready his rifle. Burles rested the barrel on the window ledge, motioning for Peachy to stay clear.

Peachy traced the bubbles of the thing under the water, as frightening memories of what he had come to believe was a nightmare crowded into his head. Alligator eyes just below the surface, the creature swam right up to the stairs and lifted itself slowly from the chilly water.

Pointed snout turning every direction as if sniffing the air for danger, the two-legged rat creature crouched below the top stair. It searched Water Lane, scanning right and then left. Seeing no one, it tiptoed, dripping, over to the wall where the code was chalked. Pausing momentarily to decipher the message, it turned and scurried back.

Burles followed the creature with his sights, his gun tight to his shoulder. Moments later, Captain Frith appeared through the portcullis of the Bloody Tower, carrying the sack filled with the fake jewels. He hesitated, looking from side to side, then leaned down to pass over the bag.

The creature reached a thickly gloved hand from the water. Frith hesitated again, glancing up and catching a glimpse of the long barrel of the rifle pointing right at him.

What happened next was so rapid that Peachy again thought it was a vision that vanished into thin air. The giant rat accepted the sack of jewels, then in a slick motion, tossed a coil of hose or cable around Frith's neck and dragged him backward into the water. Warder Burles stood in consternation, alternately raising and lowering his rifle. There was no target.

Peachy watched as across Water Lane, atop St. Thomas's Tower, Holmes jumped to his feet. A trail of bubbles heading back out to mid-channel was all that remained of the apparition of the giant rat, or of Captain Frith.

"To the boats!" Holmes cried, waving his arm for all to see. "After them!"

————

By the time the Baker Street Brigade had assembled on Tower Wharf, two steam-powered police boats awaited them. Holmes, Danny, and Peachy boarded one, while Duff and Walter Gladstone joined Police Inspector Avery on the other. Both vessels were crowded with policemen as well.

Steam pressure already up, the engines chuffed and smoked as the short, low-hulled ships pulled away in pursuit of Van Rorin and his gang. The police vessels were surely faster than the one on which the criminals sailed, but the order was to follow, not to overtake. Holmes had explained, "Should we capture them on the river, the criminal ring would not be complete and the counterfeiters and the stolen treasures would surely slip through our fingers. We must follow and observe."

The two police craft traveled in a flanking formation along each bank of the river. They were unmarked and in the dark could be taken as ferryboats should Van Rorin look back. Giving Van Rorin's vessel room to feel unpursued, Holmes ordered his fleet to keep back one-quarter of a mile, while he kept watch through his field glasses.

"Wiggins," Holmes said, "sit toward the bow and watch their ship for any sudden changes in course. Should they make any, we'll have to veer off to avoid being detected. These are desperate men and dangerous. They have silenced the one they believed was the only witness to their crime, but they will not hesitate to kill again."

Walter Gladstone looked toward Van Rorin's boat ahead of them to check on the progress. "No change," he said.

"No change," Duff repeated.

Gladstone turned to his right to see Holmes's boat skirting the water's edge on the far side of the channel. "No change," he said again.

"No change," said Duff, pleased with the game. "What do you say now?"

Whatever Gladstone would have replied was cut short when the engine sputtered and the boat lost headway. The deceleration was so sudden that the wake rushed up behind them and lapped over the stern. "What is it?" Gladstone demanded.

"No change?" Duff ventured. But he was wrong.

"We don't know, sir," a crewman called. "We're working on it." The boat settled dead in the water. Duff saw the other police boat slow and turn in their direction.

From the crewman came the report, "It's the boiler, sir. She's sprung a leak."

"How long to repair?" Inspector Avery asked.

"Not at all, sir. We can't work metal aboard the boat."

"Drat!" Gladstone yelled. "Is there nothing we can do?"

"No sir, we'll have to be towed ashore."

Gladstone ran his fingers through his hair and sat down on a crate. Holmes's boat circled near.

"Ahoy! What's the trouble?" a seaman called from the other ship.

Avery stood and shouted, "The boiler's sprung a leak!"

Holmes came to the railing of his boat. "Are you taking on water?" Peachy heard him yell.

One of the mates shouted that they were not, and Holmes retreated a step to confer with his boat's captain. "Might this boat have enough power to tow them?" he asked.

"Yes, sir," the captain said, "but only at full power, which means if the one we're following bolts, we'll not be able to keep up."

"It's a necessity that we try, captain. We must bring all the manpower we can." Holmes's boat headed directly for Gladstone's, then turned sharply to come alongside. "Avery and Gladstone," Holmes shouted, "bring your bowlines forward, we're going to tow you and continue after them." A minute later, the two boats were tied together.

"Proceed, captain," Holmes said, looking forward to Van Rorin's vessel, now just a speck in the darkness.

As the procession of ships neared the Isle of Dogs, the river turned sharply to the right and Peachy lost sight of the other boat. It worried him to think the plan had brought them this close, but might still fail.

Peachy was looking aft, toward Duff aboard the other boat, when they passed the Surrey Commercial Docks. Without warning, a large freighter pulled from the channel into the river, directly in front of the police boats.

Forgetting the boat in tow, Holmes's captain threw the engine into reverse, avoiding the freighter, but causing an unavoidable collision between the stern of one police craft and the bow of the other. There was a shuddering crash and a loud squeal as the propeller ground into the wood. Danny winced and Peachy covered his ears.

Holmes thought fast. *With the prop damaged, we'll barely make it to shore ourselves. But with the other ship slowing us down, we'll never get there.* "Captain," he shouted, "cut them loose and shove them off, we've got to go on alone."

The captain relayed the orders to the mates and soon the second police boat drifted free again. "Avery!" Holmes called as their own damaged boat limped away. "Get to Cubitt Town and look everywhere. We'll meet there if we can!"

TWELVE

THE WOUNDED STEAMER'S engines revved loudly at full power as the damaged propeller strained to do its job. The patrol craft coasted slowly into the moorings of the Regents Canal Docks. Holmes gave Danny a hand in disembarking.

"Where did they go?" the boy asked, jumping to the dock.

"We're in luck," the detective said, lowering the heavy brass field glasses after taking a look. "Just about a half of a mile downriver. Yes, there they are, heading in near the Union Docks."

"Great," Peachy said as he vaulted over the low railing to the pier. "Let's go thrash them."

Holmes turned to the skipper. "Have everyone meet us at the Union Docks. After we track Van Rorin to his cargo ship, I'll send one of the lads back for help. First stealth, then force, is the order of the day."

Holmes and the boys made their way past a charcoal and white apartment building with huge gargoyles grinning atop the edge of the roof. Across a thick grassy lawn, they veered toward the right, following steppingstones along the side of the building.

It was a deserted part of town. Composed mainly of shipping warehouses and chandleries, not much life existed there after dark. Or, what life there was about did not go openly about its business. Desolate and dark, the area was mainly for scavengers like wild dogs and tomcats, and some scavengers in human form. Any human in the area at that hour was to be feared.

At the top of the road were cluttered alleys lined with boxes and bins. And each of the packing crates and empty barrels was home to a beggar or drunkard of the London underworld.

"Crikey," Peachy said, "too many muck-snipes and soaks about. This is a place to get a neddy between your ears right enough."

The trio jogged in single file, in and out of the crooked lanes. Unseen by the three, their progress was watched by a scruffy, bearded man. He waited in a doorway as Holmes ran past.

Smiling to himself, he made no move when Danny came trotting toward him. "Always get the last goose first," he muttered, nudging his mate awake, who was sleeping in a barrel beside him. "Ollie, look what we got comin' up the road."

Panting, Peachy lagged behind Holmes and Danny. The boy neared the hovel of the two beggars, unaware that he was the hunted.

When Peachy drew even with the doorway, the first man dived out to tackle him. Peachy jumped to the side, dodging his attacker. The man circled as if he were a bull, charging Peachy once more. Peachy yelled for help.

Hearing the sound, Danny stopped to see what was

the matter. Like a prizefighter, Peachy crouched low and raised his guard. Out of the corner of his eye, he could see other lurkers waiting the slightest slip and he knew he had to get away quickly. As the man rushed in again, Peachy swung hard, aiming right at the man's nose. With a load smack the blow connected, echoing the sound of a dropped egg.

Ollie appeared, brandishing a knife. "Cut you good, I will," he threatened.

"Mr. Holmes!" Danny yelled.

Holmes, racing ahead, was nearing the Royal National Life Boat Institution when he heard the commotion behind. Instantly sizing up the situation, he drew a small caliber revolver from his coat pocket and fired it into the air. Three sharp cracking noises and jets of flame split the night air. All the alley dwellers froze in terror, then scattered and disappeared. Danny and Peachy ran after Holmes, that particular danger overcome.

————

But the shots had also put Van Rorin on the alert. Ahead of Holmes and the boys, at the Union Docks, Van Rorin's men unloaded the last of their gear from the river steamer. At the noise of the revolver, Van Rorin sent half his cronies into positions of defense.

One of Van Rorin's accomplices, hidden behind a stack of packing crates, spotted Holmes as he approached. Aiming his pistol, the man fired a single shot, puncturing the detective's side. Holmes fell like a tree. Colliding with the ground, his gun went skidding away and he lay helpless on the rounded cobblestones.

Peachy and Danny dove to their bellies and crawled inside a crate, concealing themselves in the shadows. They had not yet been noticed by Van Rorin's gang.

"So, Mr. Holmes," Van Rorin proclaimed, "you were quicker than I expected. But not quick enough, it seems."

Holmes winced, groaning in pain from a messy but not deep gouge in his side. Blood ran from his cupped fingers. "It's over, Van Rorin," the investigator said through clenched teeth. "Inspector Avery and Gladstone are on to you."

Van Rorin turned to his men and said, "You hear that, lads? This wounded duck tells us *we* are the ones in trouble." His mocking comment was followed by the laughter of the men. "Well, then," he said, looking back at Holmes on the ground, "we'll just have to hurry along, and take you as our hostage." Van Rorin snorted evilly. "Pick him up. It looks like we got another piece of valuable cargo to take to the Lime House dock."

————

Peachy and Danny lay motionless, watching from inside the box as two of Van Rorin's men picked up Holmes.

"What are we gonna do, Danny?" Peachy whispered anxiously.

"We'll just have to follow them," Danny answered. "Shhh, one of them is coming this way."

"See if anyone else is lurking out there," Van Rorin ordered a heavyset brute of a man.

The bearlike figure strutted down the dark street, scanning from side to side. The boys held their breath when the man drew up right alongside the crate they were under, but the thug turned and yelled, "I don't see no one."

"Come on, then," Van Rorin commanded, swinging his arm and pointing up the street to where a sign on a gate read *Lime House Dockyard.*

Peachy and Danny waited for Van Rorin and his men to pass though the gate and enter the dockyard before they breathed again. Danny climbed from their wood-slatted hiding place, helping Peachy up. "Come on, Peachy, we've got to save Holmes," he said, as if there were no doubt.

"How are we going to get past that?" Peachy inquired, looking up at the fifteen-foot-high fence that surrounded the shipyard.

"There's got to be another way in," Danny said confidently.

A light went on in Peachy's head. "I know, the waterside," he suggested.

"The water?" Danny questioned. "Do you mean swim in?"

Peachy nodded slowly. "If we have to, but we may be able to get 'round the blooming fence without getting wet."

Peachy and Danny followed the barrier to the corner. Turning it, they headed west toward the river, only to discover that the unclimbable fence continued thirty feet or so out into the dark, swiftly flowing stream. Swimming did not seem to be a possibility after all.

"Crikey," Danny said with disappointment, "now what?" Danny and Peachy looked around the port for something they might use to climb over.

"There's nothing here," Danny cried desperately.

"Look," Peachy said, gesturing toward the dim outline of a waterside pub, "there's a boat!" The two friends scrambled down the boulders that formed the riverbank. Peachy stepped carefully into the rowboat and grasped the oars while Danny untied the mooring line.

"Shove us off," Peachy said.

Danny pushed hard, sliding the small boat over the silt and gravel, then hopped in. Trying to keep the paddles from splashing, Peachy rowed them out to where the fence turned, then aimed into the channel leading to the dockyard.

The high fence and the towering funnels and masts of countless ships made Danny feel small as the dinghy rocked back and forth. "Blimey!" he said, "this yard is huge. We'll never find them."

Peachy continued to row. "Look for a lantern down one of the slips."

"There's someone down there," Danny said, indicating the third set of docks. There a medium-sized oceangoing steamer belched glowing sparks from its smokestack. "Must've thrown on the coal."

"Too right; gettin' up steam for leavin'. Must be them. Wouldn't no one do that in the middle of the night if they was square-rigged." Peachy let the boat drift over to a ladder at the end of the long pier, then climbed up the ladder while Danny tied up the boat.

Peering over the top, Peachy had a clear view of men toting bundles and crates, the ship, *The Star of Sunda,* and the plank used to load the cargo. "I see Van Rorin," he whispered down to Danny, "and they're loading Holmes right now."

"Is he walking?" Danny asked with concern.

"No, they're carrying him," Peachy answered. "One of us should go get Gladstone and the police. I'll stay here and keep watch. I'll be the stall until you get back."

Danny nodded as he pushed the boat off. "You be careful. I'll go get the heavy artillery."

"For Holmes," Peachy concluded.

"For Holmes," Danny echoed as he rowed out of sight.

Peachy hurried along the rough-splintered planks of the dock. Ducking low, keeping out of sight, he moved from piling to crate till he crouched near the stern of the ship.

"Hurry it up!" Van Rorin yelled angrily, "or they will be on to us." The criminal chief's voice rang out not far from where Peachy hid.

"That's the lot," a crewman's voice responded from aboard the ship.

The *Star* roused itself still further as the revolutions of the engine were increased in preparation for getting under way. The dock vibrated with the deeper rumble of the engines before they shifted into a smooth oscillating hum.

Thick black coal smoke poured over the side of the ship, blocking Peachy's view. He was startled when one of Van Rorin's men tramped along the pier to release first the forward and then the aft dock lines. Unwrapping the heavy hawser from its figure-eight tie on the cleat, the man carelessly left it resting on the dock. Then up the gangplank the sailor went, pulling it up after him.

Peachy realized, as the pitch of the engine's idle rose further still, that this was his chance. He picked up the cable and replaced the loop over the cleat, just as the propellers were engaged. Peachy hurried back to his hiding spot once more.

Thrust was applied and the ship began to move.

Stretching the rope, which creaked as it tightened, the bow of the ship swung around into the other dock.

"Stop engines!" shouted the captain. "What in blazes are you playing at, you blooming idiot? I ordered let go aft."

"I did, sir," the sailor said, leaning over the ship's side to peer through the smoke. "Blighter must have got caught as we pulled away."

"Clear it double-quick!" the captain yelled.

This was Peachy's chance to get aboard. Even as the deckhand was replacing the gangplank, Peachy swarmed aboard the *Star* on the mooring line. Once over the rail, he tucked himself away in a small corner filled with burlap sacks.

Peachy heard a groan and burrowed still deeper into the sacks. But when no one came near his hiding spot, he peeked out from under the heap of burlap. Half a deck away, tied up to a hatch was Sherlock Holmes. The detective appeared to be unconscious. Peachy wanted to go to the man at once, to free him. But he reasoned that he had better wait until Danny, Gladstone, and help arrived.

The minutes Peachy had gained by the trick with the mooring line passed all too quickly. There was a flurry of activity as the bow of *The Star of Sunda* was inspected for damage. It seemed that there was none, and soon the engines were powered up again, ready for departure. Peachy thought about creeping over the side and messing up the cables once more, but every time he started to crawl out from hiding there was more movement on deck and he was forced to stay put.

Soon it became painfully clear that help was not

going to arrive before the *Star* cast off; Van Rorin might not know it, but he would have two hostages instead of one.

"All lines free, sir," Peachy heard a man shout.

"About time!" Van Rorin snorted from somewhere close by.

As soon as Peachy heard the captain order, "Slow reverse," he looked around again, and seeing no one on the open deck, rushed to where Holmes was tied.

Peachy began working on the knots that bound the investigator. Holmes stirred at last, opening one eye. "Carnehan!" he hissed. "You mustn't! You'll be captured."

"Don't you worry, Mr. Holmes. You're hurt and I've got to get you out of here." A second later he had Holmes's legs freed and helped him to his feet. It was then that Peachy could see the bloodstains covering the detective's side. Holmes was weak from the injury and in need of attention. "If I don't get you off," Peachy said, "you'll die here, or they'll toss you over as soon as they are in the channel."

Toss over. The image came strongly to Peachy's mind; there was no time for anything else. The boy walked Holmes to the railing of the ship and positioned him so that they could jump together into the water, then swung one leg over.

"And where do you think you're going, Mr. Holmes?" Van Rorin said mockingly from behind them. Peachy and Holmes turned slowly from the railing to face the barrel of a revolver. "Surely you didn't think this street mongrel could help you?" At that moment, Holmes backhanded Peachy in the chest, sending him overboard and into the water.

Peachy surfaced in the cold murk and gasped for

air. When he cleared the water from his eyes, he reached for a line that floated next to the hull. *Jump,* he silently urged Holmes . . . *jump.*

From where he swam, the boy could not see the men on the deck, but could hear their conversation.

"Very nice of you to save the boy, Holmes," Van Rorin said, "but who'll save you?"

"Jump!" Peachy sobbed, worried for the life of his friend.

"No, Carnehan," Holmes called from the deck, "I would surely drown."

"Quiet!" Van Rorin shouted. He walked to the railing and fired into the water, though he could not see Peachy below the curve of the boat. Peachy flinched, afraid if he moved, Van Rorin would fire again. "Now it's time to dispose of you, Mr. Holmes." Peachy heard a shot and sunk his head below the surface. *I can't believe it,* he thought, *Holmes is dead.* Painful, despairing moments full of thoughts of failure and loss followed, and then . . .

"Carnehan!" a familiar voice called, "don't dally down there. Swim 'round and come dry off."

"Holmes?" Peachy shouted excitedly. "Holmes, is that you?"

"Yes, of course, lad. Who else would tell you what to do?"

Peachy smiled and laughed as he swam to the ladder connected to the dock. Climbing up, he saw that Danny had arrived with Gladstone and the officers, along with Duff.

"Nice bit of shooting, Gladstone," Holmes said as he hobbled over to the group. "Thanks to Carnehan here, you arrived just in good order."

"Indeed, Mr. Holmes? That's quite a compliment coming from you," Gladstone replied.

The officers busied themselves arresting the crewmen on board the ship. "And you, Nels Van Rorin," Inspector Avery said to the wounded gang leader, "I arrest you in the name of the Crown for theft of Crown property and for the murder of one Captain Ronald Frith."

EPILOGUE

IT WAS THE DAY after the celebration of Queen Victoria's Golden Jubilee. The ceremony, full of pomp and circumstance, lords and ladies, titles and formality, had taken place inside the centuries-old structure of Westminster Abbey.

But this day was for the common people; more importantly, for the children of London. Thirty thousand of them gathered in Hyde Park to see the queen arrive in her open-topped carriage, waving to her subjects. There were speeches, poems, plays, candy, even a captive balloon that ascended and descended on a cable to the oohs and ahhs of the crowd.

Duff, along with Peachy and Danny, was there getting his share of the treats. When the red-and-blue painted balloon rose above the trees, Duff observed in a loud voice that it was Queen Victoria going up to heaven!

The queen was not expected to greet her many enthusiastic citizens personally. In fact, she accepted a gift of flowers from only one young girl, who represented the best wishes of all the schoolchildren of the realm.

Then the short, plump, bonneted figure, whose only concession to formality was that her dress was trimmed in ermine, left the stage. It was announced that she would retreat from the sun and the noise into her private pavilion, but first she made a stop in another enclosed tent, hastily erected for the purpose.

Meeting her there, escorted by Chief Yeoman Warder Gladstone and a stiff but smiling Sherlock Holmes, were Danny, Peachy, and Duff.

"And these are the three to whom we owe so much?" she asked.

"Yes, ma'am," Gladstone replied.

She accepted the bow of each boy, who had been coached in proper form by Holmes. Into each hand she pressed a gold coin. "Accept these with our thanks," she said. "They would be medals, but as you know, no word of the intended outrage must ever become public."

Peachy, Duff, and Danny nodded soberly. This was a direct order from the queen; they would keep the secret.

"And the reports of a giant creature lurking in the Tower are unfounded?" Queen Victoria asked.

"Quite, ma'am," Holmes explained. "The 'rat' was nothing more than a man in a diving suit. That is how the swap of counterfeit for genuine jewels was carried out."

"You were wounded in our service," the queen said to Holmes. "Accept our thanks also." Then she swept out of the room.

Danny, Peachy, and Duff emerged into the bright June day. All were dazzled by what had just happened. "We met the queen," Peachy exulted, "and we can't tell nobody about it!"

"Who'd believe it anyway?" Danny said. "Us meet the queen? They'd all say it was a bit of fakery or a fairy story."

"Oh no," Duff said, his eyes shining, "it was real, right enough. She was genuine!"

GLOSSARY

A almsman—a beggar

B bagman—the one who carries stolen goods
barker—a gun
bender—a sixpence
blighter—a derogatory reference to an object
blimey—an expression of surprise
bloke—a man
blooming—stupid, disgusting; impolite descriptive word
Bobbie—policeman
bookie—one who accepts bets from gamblers
burke—to strangle
buzzer—a pickpocket or common thief

C cased for a pull—studied as a pickpocket victim
cat's paw—an accomplice to a crime
chap—man
chavvy—street brat
cheerio—a friendly greeting
chit—a bookmaker's receipt for a wager
cool—to notice or observe

cor—an expression of surprise

crikey—an expression of surprise

cripes—an expression of surprise or disbelief

crusher—a guard

D dodgy—suspicious

doing a bit of the soft—making counterfeit money

dotty—crazy

F flimp—a pickpocket

G give over—quit, give it up

glocky—crazy or unreliable

granny—to know or guess

gull—to fool someone

H hansom cab—two-wheeled carriage pulled by one horse

having you on—kidding or fooling

hawk—to sell, especially on the street

hawser—a hole in the ships hull for a rope to pass through

J jack—another name for a fellow or a man

K knap—steal

L leave off—stop or quit

lollygagging—loitering

lurk—hide or a hiding place

M mace—a weapon (a club)

mate—friend or pal

muck-snipe—homeless beggar

N neddy—a club or blackjack

newsie—a paperboy

nose—an informant

not half—an expression of disagreement

O oy—a word to get attention, like Hey!

P patter—attention-getting talk by street vendors

Peeler—a policeman

prog—food

Q queue—a line of people
R rampsman—a mugger
   raven—a lookout
   ream—right, proper, genuine
   right-o—an expression of agreement
   rookery—a bad neighborhood, full of crime
S scuppered—beaten severely
   shindy—a fight
   skip—to run away from or run out on
   snaffle—to steal
   soak—a drunkard
   square-rigged—proper, correct
   sticky bun—a sweet roll
   swell—one who dresses like a gentleman
T tanner—a sixpence
   terrier crop—prison haircut
   too right—an expression of agreement
   translator—a dealer in stolen goods
   turned—became an informant
W wizard—wonderful, marvelous

Historical notes

1) The Tower of London—the name is misleading. The Tower of London is not just a single tower. Instead it is a castle, a fortress, a barracks, and a number of other things and contains twenty towers as well as walls, battlements, and two chapels.

2) Yeoman Warders—there are two sets of guards at the Tower of London. The yeoman warders are military men who have retired to the Tower as permanent caretakers. There are also regiments of guardsmen who receive temporary assignments to patrol the Tower.

3) English money—In 1887 there were fifteen different coins in use. The basic units were the *penny* or *pence,* of which twelve made a *shilling,* and twenty shillings made a *pound* (the pound coin was called a *sovereign).* Other common coins were the *half crown,* equal to thirty pence (two-and-a-half shillings) and the *crown,* equal to sixty pence (five shillings).